The Ledger

A Story of Redemption

By Lucy Bella Donna

The Ledger

A Story of Redemption

Published by

Scribblers Press

9741 SE 174th Place Road, Summerfield, Florida 34491

Printed by

Trinity Press

3190 Reps Miller Road, Suite 360, Norcross, Georgia 30071

Library of Congress Control Number: 2020909006

Lucy Bella Donna, 06/01/2020

The Ledger - A Story of Redemption - Lucy Bella Donna

Summary: This story is a work of fiction. The characters, events, places, entities, and names, were imagined and created by the Author for fiction. Any resemblance to persons living or dead is coincidental. Authentic places, locations, known names and entities were mentioned to give a sense of reality to the Story.

ISBN: 9781950308200

DEDICATION

To Gram.....still missing you after 68 years.

To my Grandchildren, a light in my life.

ALYSSA...A HEAD ON HER SHOULDERS, ...WISDOM The Spirit of Abigail...*"and she was a woman of good understanding, and of a beautiful countenance"*...1 Samuel...Chapter 25, Verse 3. Scripture verse taken from the KING JAMES BIBLE (KJV) THOMAS NELSON BIBLE. Public Domain

HANNAH...A VOICE LIKE AN ANGEL...*"Then I looked and heard the voice of many angels, numbering thousands upon thousands"*... Revelation...Chapter 5, Verse 11. Scripture verse taken from THE HOLY BIBLE, NEW INTERNATIONAL VERSION (NIV)... Copyright 1973, 1978, 1984, 1986 by Zondervan, all rights reserved. ZONDERVAN Library of Congress Catalog Card Number 73-174297. Used by permission of Zondervan.

SARAH...ALWAYS MAKES ME LAUGH....LAUGHTER IS THE BEST MEDICINE...*"A merry heart does good, like medicine..."* Proverbs...Chapter 17, Verse 22. Verse taken from the NEW KING JAMES VERSION (NKJV) Copyright 1982 by Thomas Nelson, Inc. Used by permission. All rights reserved.

LEAH...SOFT, SWEET, SENSITIVE...A HEART OF GOLD. *"But the wisdom that is from above, is first pure, then peaceable, gentle, and easy to be intreated, full of mercy and good fruits"*...James...Chapter 3, Verse 17. Scripture verse taken from the KING JAMES BIBLE (KJV) THOMAS NELSON BIBLE. Public Domain.

ACKNOWLEDGEMENT

The intention of writing this book was a hope in reaching young adults. It is a light mystery with a story of redemption. Our God is the God of second chances.

I wish to thank all the members of the Scribblers Christian Writers Group for the encouragement they gave me to go on with my project. To Charles De Andrade, Author of books, including The Steward Series, Founder of Scribblers Writing Groups and Scribblers Press Publishing, thank you for encouraging us to use our life's experiences and make them come alive in fiction and non-fiction. I send my gratitude to Randi D. Ward, Award Winning Author and Teacher of English Literature, for her time, encouragement and her editing skills and to Marlene Ratledge Buchanan, Author, Humorist and Columnist for the Gwinnett Citizen, for her advice, humor and incentive not to give up. To Mike Owens and Leda Still, our Leaders of the Lilburn Chapter, I am grateful for their guidance and encouragement to carry on. A special Thank You to Bridgett Joyce, Graphic Designer for Trinity Press, for her ingenuity and creative design skills in turning an idea into a reality. I especially thank her for her kindness and patience in seeing that my project reach its goal. To all my Family, Church Ladies, and Dear Friends who put up with my messy home for so long, you are the best. THANK YOU! Most of all, I thank my Lord and Savior Jesus Christ who paid the price and died, so that we might live.

He said tell them about Me.

"How then shall they call on Him in whom they have not believed?
And how shall they believe in Him of whom they have not heard? And
how shall they hear without a preacher?"
Romans 10:14 (ASV)

~ CHAPTER ONE ~

The Ledger

Niki Hughes placed her face **flush** to the floorboards. Her slender frame lay prone, as she peeked through the narrow space between the door and the flooring. Her body was as still as the stagnant leaves on the oaks surrounding the Purple Cottage Bed and Breakfast. It was 2 a.m.

Niki's eyes widened as the approaching footsteps became louder. The second-floor landing was less than ten feet away, within her eye range. Only the door separated her from the tips of the rubber soles that had now become visible. She lay motionless as she watched the intruder stop for several seconds and continue up the stairs to the next level. Placing her finger over her lips, she motioned to her mother not to speak. Her heart pounded until her porcelain complexion turned to scarlet. A lock of her auburn hair stuck to her clammy cheek, and she brushed it aside. She remained riveted to the floor.

TWO DAYS EARLIER

CAMWOOD TWO MILES—Niki could hardly read the twisted sign that stood at the edge of the dirt road. Her yellow Hyundai convertible, its black top down, beamed in the early August sun.

"Sorry for the late start," she turned toward her mother.

"Don't give it a second thought." Sarah leaned back and closed her eyes. "I'm glad to get away." She dozed off.

Niki smiled and lowered the volume on the radio. Her green print blouse clung to her back. Hoping to get some relief, she shifted her body, picked up her water bottle and gulped three quarters of it down, before placing it back in its holder. A black crow swooped across her windshield and landed on top of a wooden pole across the road. *Are you as hot as I am, little guy?* she thought.

It was late afternoon when they crossed over Beacon Bridge. A warm sea breeze filled their nostrils. Sarah, half asleep, inhaled the salty air. It revived her enough to sit. "I'm in the mood for seafood."

Niki ignored Sarah's craving and continued to drive east. She saw the western sky in the rear view mirror turn from tangerine to a light crimson. A wrong turn landed the car on an unpaved road. Sparkles of color encased in the gravel beneath danced before her eyes. It reminded her of younger days and how she and her best friend Diana would jump rope on the glistening pavement in front of her home until the streetlamps went on. *Whatever happened to Diana?*

Inviting her mother to come along had been a last minute decision for Niki. A three night stay at a small B&B seemed a perfect time to catch up on the things their work schedule had prevented.

The Purple Cottage Bed and Breakfast was located two miles east of Camwood's city proper. Niki had been there some years before with co-workers and enjoyed the company of its owner Adelaide. Since that summer, she and Adelaide had become friends, corresponding several times a year.

"Hand me the map on the dashboard. Will you, Mom?" Unsure of the local streets arranged in clusters surrounding the narrow canals, she took the coffee stained map from Sarah. Pulling over to the side, she followed the outline she had drawn of the town and its areas closest to the water. "One more bridge to cross," she said triumphantly. She found her way to the main road and onto the old wooden bridge. They could hear the planks creek beneath the car.

"Could we get out of here?" Sarah pled.

"Relax, Mom. I need to turn left at the fork. Ramsey Place crosses that road. We'll be there in five minutes."

It took several cruises up and down Ramsey before Niki spotted the pastel-colored door. The old inn was set back from the other homes. Hidden from the view of passersby, it was surrounded by high trees and heavy shrubs.

Unpacking the car was easy—lugging the suitcases up the shaky steps was a challenge. They entered the foyer and were enveloped by an eerie silence. "Anybody here?" Niki called out. Still silence.

A recollection of four years earlier caused Sarah to wince. Niki had taken her to a small mid-western town for the weekend. The hotel was full due to a delayed convention. The two women were hustled off to an annex and spent half the night trying to sleep through the sound of loud shuffling in the room above. It seemed there was a guest who was unhappy with the furniture arrangement. Sarah groaned as the image faded. "Anybody here?" she echoed.

"Adelaide told me our room is on the second floor," Niki said, approaching the stairs.

As they reached the upper landing, Niki noticed only one door had been left open. She elbowed her way into the room. "This must be it. I almost forgot how beautiful these rooms were." She dropped her luggage in the first available spot.

Before Sarah could respond, a voice coming from the staircase was heard. "Goodness, I didn't expect you so soon. How was your trip?"

Inheriting it from her father and grandfather, Adelaide Wilcox had been the proprietor of the Purple Cottage Bed and Breakfast for over twenty years. She was a tad under 6 foot, slim, blond, and middle aged. She had never married or bore children. Her guests became her offspring, and she doted on them with delight. "I was out back tending to the tomatoes," she was holding a small shovel in one hand. "I didn't hear the car pull up." She brushed her dyed hair back. "I see you two ladies have begun to settle in. I'll go and put the kettle on, and you can tell me all about your trip. We almost have a full house now that you've arrived."

Detecting the excitement in Adelaide's voice, both women smiled. Sarah stopped unpacking and walked over to the windows that took space on most of the south wall. A pair of heavy chintz drapes hung from the twelve-foot-high ceilings. She felt the lace curtains hanging in-between. After a thorough inspection, she convinced herself there was enough privacy to ignore the shades rolled up at the top. She returned to her suitcase.

Two beds were placed on the opposite wall, each a different size. They had no trouble deciding which bed they would be most comfortable in. A small mahogany table stood near the door. On it lay a tiny crystal dish holding the calling cards of some local merchants, advertising everything from gourmet eateries to foreign movie theatres and expensive boutiques. Niki reminded herself to take a few.

"Mom, would it be okay if I showered first?" She walked toward the bathroom, "I'm a mess after the long drive."

"Go ahead. I'll finish unpacking." Sarah proceeded to line her clothing on the bed in categories of shirts first, skirts, shorts, and underwear, color coding her outfits before hanging them up.

Niki found her way to the bathroom located midway through a long corridor. Opening the linen closet, she chose the softest towel she could find and placed it on the edge of the porcelain tub. Black and white diamond shaped tiles covered the walls and reappeared as trim in the shower area. A mirrored medicine cabinet etched with flowers hung on the far wall over a pedestal sink. She hung her robe on a hook attached to the bathroom door, undressed, and set her clothes down on a small stool. She turned the faucet to its warmest setting and immersed herself into the bath and closed her eyes. Soft music streamed its way into the partially open window. Niki smiled as warm steam invaded the room and snuck out into the narrow hallway.

Sarah emptied her suitcase and threw herself onto the bed. It didn't take long for Niki to appear wrapped in her robe with a turban of terrycloth twisted about her head. "Go ahead, Mom, your turn."

The curtains swayed as a light breeze drifted in through the windows. The smell of lavender crept its way up the brick wall into the room. Niki gratefully inhaled its fragrance. Walking over to the old windows, she drew the drapes. She noticed the windows were absent of sills, and the loosely pried screens posed a threat should anyone lean on them too hard. *I'll have to tell Mom not to lean.*

As she gazed about the room, her eyes were drawn to the watercolors hung symmetrically on the far wall. There were four in all, portrayed by local artists—high-lighting the town's attractions. She made a mental note to visit each one. A double burner sat on the round table in a corner near the door. It held a glass coffee pot, several coffee filters, a box of tea bags and some sugar packets. A half-filled can of ground coffee had been placed next to the burner along with a jar of powdered creamer. Anxious to explore, she decided to wait until dinner to get her coffee fix.

Sarah returned to their room. Drops of water trailed behind. "I see you're ready. Why don't you go and chat with Adelaide, I'll only be a few minutes."

Niki slipped out the door and down the staircase. Half-way into her descent, she yelled over her shoulder, "Don't lean on the screens. They're loose."

Wise for her 30 years—at least those closest to her thought—Niki tended to hold back before making a judgment. She weighed all the facts, said little, and listened much, unlike her mother who was known for her knee-jerk reactions. Considered pleasant to look at, with high cheek bones and plum colored eyes, her sun-kissed face, inherited at birth, was accepted and rarely covered up with makeup. She jokingly blamed it on her grandmother's side. Gentle in nature, she maintained a sense of humor without being sarcastic. She would be a great catch if the right man came along. Unbeknownst to her mother, she wasn't even looking.

Camwood, in Niki's mind, was both quaint and preppy. The houses that lined the land east of the riverbanks were Victorian in style with lovely gardens out back. Other homes, closer to the canals, were raised on stilts, yet the locals managed to plant some vegetation by installing systems that kept the wet soil drained. They were proud of their marsh marigolds, planted from seedlings, and enjoyed the summers when they competed for the tallest swamp roses. In the town, the sidewalk cafes near the water's edge were dotted with colorful painted tables that had chessboards carved into their cement tops. Students from a nearby college would visit on the weekends to challenge the old-timers to a game and often lose. Sometimes the games could last for hours while other times it would take only minutes before someone cried "Checkmate." Small stop clocks, courtesy of the owners, were kept at each table for the players to use. Each player would hit the button after making his move, causing the intermittent rings to sound like a strange symphony when all the tables were occupied. Converted gas lamps stood proudly up and down Main Street and displayed their lights over the gray cobblestones. In the warmer months the street musicians would play under them until dawn to the delight of the younger crowd.

Camwood offered a variety of people with various ethnic backgrounds. Spending an afternoon at one of the cafes on the Town Square was on the top of Niki's list of things to enjoy.

After dressing for dinner, Niki and Sarah made a quick exit. They decided to dine at a local restaurant a short distance from the inn. Upon entering the car, it dawned on Sarah they did not sign the register. "I'll go, Mom. Wait here," Niki offered. She re-entered the small vestibule and signed the green and gold leather book propped up on a long oak table under the staircase. A vase of freshly cut wildflowers stood next to a porcelain dish that held the B&B's business cards. Niki grabbed a card, tucked it into her inside jacket pocket, and returned to the car." Seafood it is," she pulled away from the curb. Sarah grinned in victory.

The early morning light peeked through the curtains. Still half asleep, Niki rolled over on her side. The aroma of freshly baked croissants infiltrated the room. "Mom, are you awake?" Getting no response, she jumped out of bed and grabbed the large blue towel hanging on the hook of the bedroom door. Seeing her mother was still asleep, she disappeared down the hall.

Sarah opened one eye. "Smells great," she mumbled. "You go ahead. Don't worry about me. I'll catch up." Her response never reached Niki's ears.

Within forty-five minutes, the two women had showered and dressed. Niki walked over to the closet and chose a two piece red suit for that evening. As the steam lingered, she returned to the bathroom, suit in hand, and hung it on a chain attached to the shower door. She straightened the skirt and returned to the bedroom in time to hear her mother's footsteps on the back staircase." Hey, wait for me. I'm coming," Niki yelled.

Adelaide had been up for hours preparing what she took the most pride in—her breakfast buffet. Her cheerful voice cried out from behind the pantry door. "Good morning, Ladies. Did you sleep well?"

"Yes, I slept well. Thank you," Niki strolled toward the breakfast area.

"Ditto," piped Sarah. They took their seats at the table, opposite each other.

At the far end sat a middle aged man with silver hair. "I'm Harry and this is my wife Marge." He was unable to force a smile. "We're the Bernsides—we're from Phoenix." His face revealed a look of relief the introduction was over. Marge smiled a half-smile. She appeared to be subdued and a bit depressed. Niki caught the mood and no longer wondered why they sat isolated from the other guests.

"I'm Niki, and this is my mom Sarah," Niki smiled and turned toward a younger man and a boy seated on her left.

"I'm Jack Heaton, and this is my son Sean," said the middle aged man. "We saw you arrive yesterday afternoon."

"I'm happy to know you." Niki shot a glance at the Bernsides. "We chose to dine out early and get a feel of the town. We got back a little late and didn't notice anyone in the parlor."

"Did you enjoy it?" Marge asked.

"Very much." Niki stood and excused herself. With her mother following, she strolled to the buffet that was spread out on an old oak rectangular table under a large window. Salvaged from an old church, multicolored panels of stained glass filtered the morning sunlight, casting a peach glow that invaded the alcove. They filled their plates and returned to the table in time to see a robust woman with white hair enter the room. "Good morning, she said with a broad grin. "To those I haven't yet met, I'm Neva."

Neva was short in stature with a huge personality and large powder blue eyes. She kept her pure white hair short and styled behind her ears in a tight perm. On occasion she would use a blue rinse that gave her a touch of sophistication when the light hit it just right. She was baby faced, and her skin pink and unweathered as one would not expect living in a tropical island.

Neva loved to travel and was especially pleased when young

adolescents joined her tour group. Being around the youth of the world kept her lighthearted as she observed their mannerisms and style. She dressed in what she thought was stylish for her age. Although she never divulged it, she was well over eighty.

Adelaide returned to the dining room and ushered Neva to one of the empty chairs across from Niki. "Say hello to Neva, everyone. She comes to us all the way from the beautiful island of Puerto Rico. She arrived late last evening and unfortunately didn't get to meet you."

Jack leaned over the table and extended his hand. "Welcome. I'm Jack, and this is my son Sean."

"I'm pleased to meet you both." Neva smiled, and glanced at Sarah. Her smile lingered.

Sarah returned the smile. "This is my daughter Niki. We are both pleased to meet you Mrs..."

"Forgive me," My name is Pelleron, Neva Pelleron."

"Would you prefer we call you Neva?" Niki stopped the warm croissant about to slip off her plate.

"Neva is fine. In fact, I'd rather you did."

"What a lovely daughter you have, Sarah," Neva's smile broadened as she poured herself a cup of coffee and eyed her new acquaintances.

"Nicole is wiser than her 30 years would normally allow her to be." Her mother referred to Niki for the first time in years by her full name.

Noticing the Bernsides were not wanting to engage in the morning's conversation, Neva called out, "Hello down there. I'm Neva, and you are...?"

It took several moments before Harry replied. "I'm Harry Bernside, and this is my wife Marge." He forced a smile.

"Would you like to join us at this end?" Neva asked.

"We were about to leave. We had an early start this morning but thanks anyway." Harry stood and pushed his chair under the table.

The Bernsides excused themselves and dashed out of the room, leaving Neva with her thoughts about the strange pair. She chuckled softly and turned to Niki and Sarah. "Would you, Ladies, like to join me for dinner tonight? I frequent the Brass Door whenever I visit Camwood. They are always happy to see me and receive my guests. I'd be happy to pay for the taxi ride."

Waiting for a signal of approval, Niki glanced at her mother.

Sarah smiled. "We have our car with us. Yes, we'd be delighted, Neva."
Niki chimed in. "Would you like to ride with us?"

"No, thank you. I have some shopping to do in town. I was
going to take a taxi over there about six o'clock. You may drive me
home if you like."

They agreed to meet at the Brass Door that evening. Niki was
looking forward to learning more about this seasoned woman. She had
felt an instant bond with Neva, and although they never discussed it,
Sarah felt it also.

~ CHAPTER TWO ~

Harry and Marge Bernside had arrived at the Purple Cottage Bed and Breakfast, shortly after 11 a.m. After settling in, Marge threw herself across the massive four poster bed and wiped her eyes to prevent the tears that welled from falling. "I miss the grandchildren already. Why did we have to leave Phoenix in the first place? We could have used the tickets another time."

"And hurt their feelings." Harry snapped. "Let's get this over with so I can get on with my dull life."

Harry did not appreciate the gesture from their children, which included round trip tickets to Camwood, a one week stay at the bed and breakfast, theatre tickets, and car rental, but he was sensitive enough not to turn them down. His children may have been sincere in their giving and could be making amends for several ugly incidents of the past. It never dawned on him.

Harry trusted no one. His climb up the corporate ladder did not come easy. He'd been elevated to chairman of the company some years before and left behind a trail of bitter businessmen whom he had backstabbed and cheated without a second thought. He was a short stocky man of sixty-five with narrow dark eyes and low set brows. He had lost a fraction of his hair in his early thirties. Whatever was left had turned to silver. He had a way of growing one side to a longer length and tossing it over the middle of his scalp to hide the vacancy. He was ruthless, having no regard for those he stepped on to reach his pinnacle. In recent months his conscience gnawed at him, and the scene that took place prior to this trip haunted him.

It was raining that afternoon and exceptionally windy. Harry had remembered to grab his hat and umbrella as he rushed out the door to keep his 9 a.m. board meeting at corporate headquarters.

The president and vice-president of Filtrec Electronics Corp. had suspected some shareholder tampering and did not want to alarm the other board members. After delving into the corporate books, they decided to call a private meeting with Harry so they could discuss their findings. They wanted to get his take on things. They trusted their colleague and were hoping for his full support.

Harry arrived ten minutes late. He loved being late. It made him feel important to be the last one to arrive. As he entered the massive dome shaped room and studied the faces of his superiors, he sensed the outcome of the meeting would depend on him. He was confident the other members would unanimously agree to his ideas. A small twitch evolved at one corner of his mouth as he anticipated giving his well rehearsed presentation.

The two gentlemen, puffing away on their imported Havana's, were the only two members present. Harry's smile faded. "Where are the others?" He crossed the smoke filled room.

"There are no others, Harry. We need to talk to you about a serious matter. Please take a seat." The eyes of his overseers watched as he chose a seat opposite them at the end of the conference table. Their muffled voices drifted into silence.

"I'm sorry. I didn't catch that." Harry said.

"It wasn't meant for you to catch," was the response.

"Well, that being the case, good morning, Gentlemen. Let's get on with it. What's this all about? Where is everyone?"

The conference table was arranged to accommodate the ten board members, each place set to precision: Ten notepads, ten silver plated pens, ten glasses, and two huge water pitchers, accompanied by small plates of lemon wedges, spread out evenly across the table's broad surface.

Scott Jacobs, the company's president, spoke first. "Harry, we didn't invite you here to discuss your presentation. What we want to tell you, we tell you reluctantly."

Harry felt off balance. He held onto the conference table and eased into the black leather chair. He couldn't swallow and wished he could have a beer. He reached for one of the pitchers and poured a glass of iced water and drank half of it down before he spoke as the two men watched.

"I agree with Scott," Vice-President Benjamin Lewis said, making eye contact with Harry. "Since you have invested so much of your time and energy into this company, we wanted to present the facts to you first. More than one and a half million dollars is missing from the company funds. Someone has been funneling the money to different accounts, and we are not going to give up until we find out who is doing this."

Harry's face paled as he listened to both men describe how the books had been tampered with. He studied their faces to see if they were studying his. "We are responsible for every red cent. We owe it to our shareholders to hold the guilty person, or persons accountable. If you know anything, we appeal to you to tell us what you know. You have access to our books. Haven't you noticed the depleted funds?" Benjamin asked. "Have you had any suspicions of your own?" Harry sat stoic. Did his silence condemn him?

"Harry, are you listening?" Marge asked. "Where have you gone to?" Harry's image faded. He was grateful for the interruption. Marge left the room to call the children in peace and Harry stepped into the bathroom to shave. He snapped at her to hurry, he wanted the night to be over.

Marge Bernside was a woman of medium build in her mid-fifties with salt and pepper hair and unassuming brown eyes. She had a kind and gentle nature, so gentle her friends often wondered how she had ended up with someone like Harry. Not attractive by most standards, her smile, though not often exhibited, was considered her best feature.

After showering and changing clothes the couple walked along the narrow stone streets to a small Cabaret located near the town square. A drop of water hit the tip of Marge's nose. It caused her to gaze upward. A light drizzle fell across her face, and it felt good. Harry grabbed her arm and ushered her into the small bistro. "We forgot to take an umbrella," Marge said. "The forecast did say rain. We may have to call a cab." As the Hostess guided the couple to a window seat, the soft rainfall morphed into a downpour, and Marge thought of how fortunate they were to have timed their walk so perfectly.

~ CHAPTER THREE ~

Jacobi (Jack) Heaton and his son Sean had arrived shortly after the Bernsides. He promised this trip to Sean as a reward for having played a major role in helping his soccer team to victory at Milltown High School. Each player received a trophy, but it was Sean's last play that scored the win.

Jack was an introvert of sorts, a tad over six feet, and handsome with hazel eyes. His thick dark hair, slightly graying at the temples, gave him a distinguished look, and along with his light eyes and chiseled face he became a target for some available young and not so young females in his town who would go to extremes to catch his eye. He had a cluster of small tattoos up and down both arms that he hated and tried to hide by wearing long sleeved shirts most of the time. He called it a foolish mishap of his twenty something years. His disdain for shaving was evident. He would skip a day or two, here and there. Sean wished his father would make up his mind and grow something of substance rather than have his chin remain in limbo.

Jack was a success in the field of photography and had raised his son alone. His wife of nineteen years had left, divorcing him and marrying her high school sweetheart, leaving Sean behind. Jack took over the role of both parents, and so far he had done a good job. He remained in the mid-western county of Holland Park and opened his own studio. The town itself was a historic area that was dotted with old mills, thus the name Milltown. At present, he was dating a local woman who had commissioned him for class portraits. A teacher at a nearby elementary school, she had sought him out from the advice of a colleague who was familiar with Jack's work. His relationship with Anne proved to be a satisfying one, and he was becoming more comfortable with it as the months passed.

Sean was tall for his seventeen years. He inherited his light eyes along with his love for sports from Jack, who was at one time a volunteer coach for the Milltown Warriors baseball team. Sean belonged to the local bowling team and excelled in roller hockey. Along with his cleft chin, his reddish-brown hair was a gift from his mother's side of the family. He hated the color of his hair and once thought about dyeing it but was afraid his father would ground him for a year, so he opted out. Jack, who was proud of his son, harbored no fears as to the future he would have and uplifted him in all his endeavors, but dyeing his hair would not be one of them. Jack's only regret was Sean was without a mother or siblings to help with the encouragements.

Jack, being content in his relationship with Anne, grew more confident in his work. With his personal life in high gear, he was sure he would take some prize photos home. He preferred scenic shots as opposed to portraits and was hoping to perfect his skills in light and shadow during his stay. He knew Camwood with its parks and narrow canals would be a perfect backdrop to capture his love of nature on film.

After signing in, Jack and Sean found their way to their room located on the main level of the house. "This is neat, Dad, the fireplace is awesome." Sean stopped in front of the mahogany bookcases that flanked the stacked stones of the chimney. "I wonder if there's a hidden door behind these."

"There goes that imagination again. It was generous of Adelaide to give us the best room in the house. We must thank her. Let's get a move on, Son. I want to get some info on the boating schedules from Adelaide before dinner."

"OK, I won't be long." Sean stepped into the bathroom.

Jack unpacked, placing his shirts neatly in the bottom drawer of an old maple chest. "You take the first two drawers," he yelled in his son's direction.

Jack had brought extra film and two of his favorite cameras with him.
One had a special lens for shooting in foggy conditions. He placed it
gently on top of the high boy and threw himself across one of the beds.
He was expecting fog along the coastline that evening and was excited
to try out his new lens. He hoped to capture some of the smaller crafts
as they glided along the dusky water. Thinking of surprising Anne with
a call, he was interrupted by Sean who exited the bathroom leaving tiny
puddles along the Berber carpet.

"I hope you're not too disappointed the Warriors lost, Dad. I'm sure
they will do better next time."

"I'm not disappointed at all, Son. They'll be other games."

It was almost 8:30 p.m. when father and son found their way to a
steak house, not more than a mile from the B&B.

Neva Pelleron returned from her evening at the Brass Door after having
enjoyed the company of the Hughes women. She entered her room on
the first level, directly across from Jack and Sean's room, and tossed
her handbag onto the bed. Pulling over the old rocker resting in a small
archway by the window, she sat and began to sway. As she closed her
eyes, she envisioned a scene from her younger days. A tear trickled
down one side of her face as she reminisced about Carl and their
courtship together.

It had been love at first sight for the couple who had met on a blind date
over half a century ago. Neva recalled how Carl had called for her in a
cab because he could not afford a car of his own. Times were bad, and
although they both worked full time positions, neither was able to save
much. The cab ride was a luxury for both, but Carl was willing to spend
whatever it took to make an impression on his mystery date. It worked
because the moment Neva laid eyes on the handsome Latin, she fell head
over heels for him.

Likewise Carl was impressed with Neva. After a year of courtship,
they married in a quiet ceremony at a small church in the fishing village
of Fajardo, not far from the El Yunque Rain Forrest. They settled in
the beachfront community of Ocean Ridge, less than two hours away.
Carl had invested the little money he had in tobacco, and after several

years, along with his father, they were able to buy a small plantation. With the help of local laborers, life began to thrive for the couple. They experienced a touch of upper-class blessings until the death of Carl's father, Juan. Carl began making poor choices. After the hurricanes hit, he invested in bad deals and the business slowly crumbled. During that time, Neva researched the tobacco industry. Determined to help in any way she could, she traveled throughout South America and Europe meeting with the cooperate heads of the more renowned companies and charming her way into their private sessions and most intimate conversations. She kept journals containing all the needed information to help Carl put his company back on the A-list. As the company began to thrive again, investors from all over the globe bought stock in the Eastern Central Tobacco Corp. After Carl's death, Neva was free to run the business as she pleased. Because of the wise choices she made, she was known as one of the wealthiest women on the island.

As the old wooden chair swayed, Neva's thoughts were interrupted by the sound of footsteps in the hallway. She sat and listened, hoping the sounds would cease at her door. Any visitor capable of erasing her melancholy would have been welcomed. No one came.

The Camwood Lake was murky and cold. The fish were freshwater. The full moon shone. It created shadows that moved swiftly with the soft, rippling waves. "Better to catch fish at night, isn't it Dad?"

"Sometimes," Jack answered. He raised his pole and cast his line into the inky water. Sean followed and waited. The water reflected the sky's light, like a dark cracked mirror, as the moon ducked in and out of the clouds.

"Catfish come out at night, right Dad?" Sean asked, eager to learn.

"They do Son, in fact, they are more aggressive at night. Maybe you'll get a strike."

Jack and Sean returned from their night of fishing. The few bass they caught were offered to Adelaide who gratefully took them. They passed by Neva's door and Sean struggled to stifle a cough in hopes of not disturbing the elderly woman he and his father had met at breakfast.

"Hope you're not catching anything, Son." Jack was concerned.

"I'm ok, Dad, a little tired. It's nothing a good night sleep can't cure." Closing the door behind them, the two were unaware of the loneliness Neva was experiencing in her room. Within half an hour all activity on the first floor had ceased.

~ CHAPTER FOUR ~

Niki gazed at the chandelier that illuminated the oak paneled dining room of the Brass Door. Despite its grandeur, the room maintained a rustic simplicity which she admired. The three women were ushered to a table in the Garden Room, which was partitioned off at the rear of the building. Neva was known and well-liked by most of the staff, and those who knew her would accommodate her in any way they could. She insisted on privacy.

"I'm delighted to see you again, Rita. It's been awhile. Hasn't it?" Neva addressed her server.

"Yes, it has, Mrs. Pelleron. Please don't let it be so long between visits. We missed you."

"Take your time." Rita handed each woman a menu, leaving them to decide. She disappeared into the main dining room.

The evening passed quickly for the mother and daughter. Niki was like a sponge and soaked up every ounce of wisdom from this seasoned woman. "Can you tell me more about your husband?" Niki asked Neva during dessert.

Sipping her iced tea, Sarah was eager to hear, and tried to grasp every word. "Yes. How did you meet him?"

"It's not so important how I became Mrs. Pelleron. What's important is how Mr. Pelleron became the man he was." There was a hint of humility in her voice.

Neva decided she would first reveal the good aspects of their relationship. She described Carl's hard work and perseverance of forty plus years before telling of how she had to rescue the company from going bankrupt. "My husband began small, growing his plants on the slopes of Puerto Rico in the east. As the business took off, he would buy more land, and after many years most people on the island had heard of his success. As demands for Tobacco grew, orders kept pouring in from the mainland, so much so that we could hardly keep up. In those days the business would reach a peak, only to be wiped out when a hurricane hit. When the crops were wiped out, he would begin again. He never complained," she added. "When the last hurricane hit, Carl had had it. That's when I stepped in. I wanted to help in any way I could. He wanted to surrender—he needed guidance." Her voice turned brittle, and her eyes became moist. Embarrassed, she raised her tone. "I guess I inherited my tenacity from my grandmother. We had big plans, Carl and I." She paused for a moment, "they included a large family, but we never did have children." Her mouth became slightly twisted. "Oh, we tried alright. I knew deep down it was inevitable—we were not destined to be parents."

Niki and Sarah exchanged glances. "Neva, why didn't you adopt?" Niki asked.

"Niki, how rude," Sarah interrupted. "What made you ask something so personal?"

The heat rose in Niki's cheeks. "Please forgive me, Neva. Mom is right. I shouldn't have pried like that."

"That's quite alright Dear," Neva accepted the apology. She leaned forward and patted Niki's hand. She avoided the question.

The conversation went on into the night. Niki wished she had taken a notebook with her to write the little pearls of wisdom she had gleaned from their encounter. "It's been a lovely evening thanks to the good company," Sarah said. "We can't thank you enough for tonight."

Niki echoed her mother's sentiment. "I hope we see each other again before we leave."

Sarah reached for her handbag. Catching the attempt, Neva shook her head. "It's my treat. Remember? I'll have none of that," she chided, and motioned to Rita to bring her the check. The two women thanked their new friend for her hospitality. If Niki had her way, she would have stayed for hours. For the sake of both ladies she thought it best to call it a night and offered Neva a ride back to the B&B.

Niki stepped out of the shower and towel dried her hair. She returned to the bedroom wearing the new pajamas she had bought at Bigelow's Dept. Store, and jumped into bed. "Leave some music on, Mom. It'll help me fall asleep," she instructed. Turning the dial, Sarah stopped at a soft instrumental station.

"How's this?"

As the whisper of gentle music filled the room, Niki disappeared beneath the covers. "Perfect," she replied, "just perfect," and drifted off.

~ CHAPTER FIVE ~

Joe Balboa parked in the southwest corner of the parking area. He slid out of his seat, and stepped onto the pavement. He left the police car door open as if he was preparing for a quick departure. His steps were swift and heavy. He walked in the direction of the old red brick building located at the opposite end of the lot and stopped to gaze over his shoulder several times. He pulled a handkerchief from his back pocket, wiped away the large droplets on his forehead, and stood before the entrance of an old paper mill. Facing the glass door, flanked by two massive windows, he stared at his reflection for a few seconds then focused on the image beyond his own. His eyes followed the small tan Toyota that proceeded through the rear gate into the driveway. It stopped no more than twenty feet from him. His muscular frame remained still. A figure stepped out of the car and walked toward him. The man was short in stature. He was Asian. His long, dark hair pulled back in a tight ponytail, shined in the half moon light. He was carrying a brown paper bag in one hand and a grey satchel in the other. Without speaking, he approached the officer and handed him the paper bag. Still clinging to the satchel he walked with him toward the police car. Joe placed the bag on the front seat and stepped to the rear of the car and lifted the trunk. He placed the carry-on in the front compartment and inspected its contents. Plastic bags of pure white powder, five in all, were sealed and marked with numbers. He removed the bags and handed the case back to his comrade. The two men shook hands. Joe grasped his hand a little tighter. They parted without saying a word.

Once again he was alone. The humidity lingered into the night. Still sweating, he walked over to the dumpster adjacent to the old mill. He lifted two large refuse bags out of the receptacle and placed them over the contraband. He slammed down the trunk in time to see another police vehicle enter the driveway. The male driver and a tall, dark-skinned female with black shoulder length hair stepped out of the car. Both were dressed in full uniform. They greeted Joe and spoke for several minutes. Thinking they may have heard voices, the trio glanced upward. Their eyes focused on the upper story windows of the Purple Cottage Bed and Breakfast, but they failed to see the pair of eyes staring back at them.

Niki had heard the tan Toyota when it entered the driveway. She watched as the shorter figure approached the larger man and extended his hand to him. She could tell he was Asian. She gasped as she witnessed the transactions between them. She approached her mother's bed and gently shook her. "Mom, get up," she whispered.

Sarah sat and rubbed her eyes. "What is happening, Niki?"

"Mom, something is going on down there."

"Down where?"

"In the yard, beneath our window—a police officer, but he's not acting like one."

"Niki, go to bed. If he's a police officer, I'm sure he's only taking a break."

Niki crouched between the beds and crawled back to the window. Peeking through the small opening in the curtains, she continued to eye her suspect. She watched as the second car pulled away, and another entered the parking area. She remained frozen. She saw the two officers exit their patrol car and walk toward Joe. He didn't glance up. Had he expected them?

The moonlight shone onto the police vehicle, and the local precinct's numbers were visible on its side. Niki noticed the approaching male was much shorter than the female who was following close behind. They shook hands with Joe and spoke in loud voices. Hearing sounds coming from the second story window they stared up at the B&B.

"They heard the music, Mom. I know they did." Niki's voice sounded as if she were talking through a 30's vintage fan. She could hear her heartbeat. "We are leaving here first thing in the morning."

Sarah, now fully awake, tried to calm her daughter.

Niki didn't respond. She heard laughter, followed by the sound of engines starting. Overcome by an eerie feeling, she whispered to her mother, "if they suspect someone saw them, they will be back."

Niki tossed and turned but sleep would not come. It was nearing 2 a.m. when she heard a car enter the parking lot. This time it was a four door sedan. The moon had shifted. The area was dark. She could not make out the type or the exact color of the car, yet thought it to be navy blue. Joe stepped out of the car with the man who rode with the dark-skinned female earlier. They were both dressed in civilian clothes. She could not make out what they were saying but she was positive they were the two men she had seen before. The men circled the car. Joe lifted its trunk. They hauled out two huge search lights from the car and aimed the beams up and down the side of the old mill. Satisfied the building was unoccupied they directed the beams toward the B&B.

"I knew it, Mom," she whispered, "They're back, and they know someone saw them. We are leaving now!"

"If we leave now, it will look suspicious. Adelaide will wonder what's going on, and I don't think we should involve her. Wait until morning. We will explain something came up unexpectedly and we must return home. She will understand—you know that." Still unsure of what Niki had seen, Sarah struggled to get back to sleep.

Niki knew sleep would not come. She picked up her Bible lying at the foot of the bed and began to read. Opening to one of her favorite Psalms she read, "But you, Lord, are a shield around me, my glory, the One who lifts my head high. I call out to the Lord and He answers me from His holy mountain. I lie down and sleep: I wake again because the Lord sustains me."

The sound of the front door opening could be heard from the floor above. Niki listened. Footsteps were ascending the stairs to the second level. She dropped out of bed and crawled to the bedroom door and lay flush against the floor's wooden planks. The light from the hallway illuminated the landing. Through the gap in the bottom of the door a person could be seen approaching and wearing men's sneakers. He was heading directly toward her. She took quiet little gasps of air until she found herself peering at the tips of his shoes. She held her breath. She remembered the Psalm.

After stopping at her door, the intruder ascended to the third level. Niki, too frightened to move, remained prone on the floor.

It took several minutes before Joe convinced himself nothing was amiss. He returned to the main level and disappeared into the night but not before stopping in the entrance hall to lift the leather-bound book Adelaide kept for her guests.

Niki could hear the front door close. She waited until she was safe enough to rise from the floor and whispered a prayer of thanksgiving. "We will leave in the morning," she said to Sarah, who by this time had fallen asleep.

Niki had read enough news stories to know that some law enforcement officers do not live by the standards set for them. She had watched as the heavyset man greeted the dark skinned female officer, grasping her hand as she tossed back her long black hair. The three talked for almost a quarter of an hour. Niki's thoughts were racing. Camwood's nearby Chinatown was known to be a haven for drug pushers. Maybe these officers were working undercover, but she couldn't justify the attempt to hide the bags of white powder under a collection of garbage while driving a police vehicle.

Her hope of finding sleep that night failed. Niki propped herself against two pillows and prayed throughout most of the night.

The following morning both women showered and dressed early, wanting to make a fast exit. In an odd way, Niki was sorry to be leaving. She knew she couldn't relate to Marge Bernside but thought she had found a friend in Neva.

As they entered the dining room, Niki and Sarah tried to remain alert and cheerful. Adelaide had prepared the usual European breakfast of croissants, hot from the oven, and fresh orange juice along with a variety of flavorful jams and jellies, including Niki's favorite orange marmalade. Each place was set with a glass carafe, where one could prepare and press his or her own cup of coffee. A large hand painted ceramic bowl, dotted with African Violets, stood in the middle of the table. It was filled with a medley of fresh fruit to be passed around family style. Cheese, several kinds, were cut in bite sized pieces.

As they pulled out their usual chairs and seated themselves, Harry Bernside was the first to greet them. Niki thought it to be unusual yet managed a smile. "Good morning, Ladies," Harry said. He raised his voice an octave or two. "Did anyone hear those annoying cars last night? Talk about getting some rest in a small town."

"What annoying cars?" Neva entered the dining room.

Niki's stomach sank. She wished it was Neva who had heard the cars.

"Good morning, everyone," Adelaide interrupted, "did you sleep well?" she asked in a sing-song voice.

"Sure, thanks for asking," Harry growled.

Marge, seated beside her husband, was sensitive to Adelaide's feelings and poked his side with her elbow. Harry ignored the warning and went on with his narrative. "Well it must have been sometime after midnight," he said. Our rooms are on the top floor overlooking that ghastly parking lot. The sound of a car woke me. As soon as I fell asleep again, another car came, then a third. These people decided to have a nice chat under my window."

"Did you hear anything else?" Niki asked.

"What else?"

"Well, like someone entering the house?"

"Nope, I didn't even get out of bed. I figured I'd leave the spying to my wife, but she slept through it." Harry's brows slanted inward and his eyes narrowed. "I sure as heck had a tough time getting back to sleep."

Niki was disappointed Harry hadn't heard anything to speak of. She shot a look at Sarah. Both women remained silent.

"Did you hear anything, Jack?" Harry continued to scowl and look toward the Heatons.

"Not a thing." Jack answered. "Sean was a little under the weather, so I gave him something to help him sleep. It may be a slight cold. We had a great night of canoeing on the lake—we may have overdone it."

"Feeling better today, aren't you, Son?" Neva smiled as she glanced at Sean.

"Yes, Ma'am," Sean answered, almost looking like himself. "I didn't hear anything either, I guess the medicine Dad gave me knocked me out."

Taking all of this in, Adelaide remained speechless, but one could see she was aghast at the thought her guests did not have a good night's sleep.

After finishing his coffee, Jack excused himself from the table and attempted to rise. Sean did the same, but they were interrupted by Niki. "Mom and I will be leaving Camwood today. I'm sorry to say something came up, and we have to go."

"Oh, my Lord, must you go? You haven't been here for more than two days?" Neva asked.

"Yes, we will try and make it back soon. I'm truly sorry." Neva could see her sincerity. Gazing over to Harry and Marge, Niki smiled at the odd couple. "It was nice meeting you both. I hope you enjoy your time here."

Niki and Sarah felt a sense of sadness as they said their goodbyes in the parlor of the old house. Jack and Sean, were about to spend another day exploring. They stopped on their way out to bid them farewell once again. "So sorry to see you go," Jack grabbed Niki's hand and shook it.

"I hope you accomplish what you came to do," Niki said. She turned to Sean, "Keep up the good work. I'm sure you will excel in whatever path you choose."

"I hope so," Jack interrupted, looking Sean's way. "I think we're becoming a little closer this trip. Hey, Son?"

"Sure, Dad."

The goodbyes were short. As the two women embraced Neva, tears welled up in their eyes. Exchanging contact numbers with no one else, they gave her their information. They hoped for a reunion in the future.

Finding their way to the kitchen, they approached Adelaide who had been busy preparing some fruit pies. After making their excuses for cutting their stay short, they embraced their hostess and promised to return soon. Adelaide's disappointment was evident. She managed a smile and bid the two women goodbye.

It was nearly 3 p.m. when Niki and Sarah pulled into the parking lot of the Blue Bay Diner.

"I need some coffee," Niki said. They entered through the heavy double doors.

"Smoking or non?" the hostess gave the pair a big smile.

"Non please." Sarah grinned. They were led to the non-smoking section of the little mom and pop establishment.

"I'm having second thoughts." Niki sipped from her second cup of coffee. Her tone was serious.

"What are you talking about?" Sarah asked.

"Maybe we should have gone to the Camwood Police Department before we left town. If something is going on, I should have reported it."

The smile Sarah walked in with faded. She made direct eye contact with her daughter. "What is it, Nik, I always taught you?" she asked. "Remember—when in doubt—don't. We came out of this alive, and I'm not about to jump back in. I will not have any part of this, and neither should you."

Niki played with her dessert." What if I went to one person in the department and confided in him, like a sergeant or a detective? What if I told him what I witnessed and left him on his own to deal with it as he saw fit? Mom, I have an obligation to report a crime if I witnessed it, especially if it was the law doing the crime. Think of all the young people who would be affected if I don't. I can't walk away."

Sarah reached and grabbed her purse. "You have no proof. I'm going to the Ladies Room," she responded." It will give you time to think about what you are suggesting."

Niki eyed her mother as she walked to the restroom. When she returned, Sarah sat down in the blue vinyl booth and challenged her daughter. "Did you think it over, Niki? Do you see how foolish you are acting?"

"Mom, suppose you stay in the car, and I'll go in and speak to someone. I promise I won't talk to anyone I'm not comfortable with." Niki was unyielding. Leaning over the table, she insisted, "I can't end this trip without doing the right thing."

The pair returned to the car. Sarah remained silent as Niki made a U-turn and headed in the direction of Camwood.

~ CHAPTER SIX ~

Police Headquarters was located in the historical old town on the east side of the city, two blocks west of the theatre district, and five blocks north of Chinatown. The department was headed by Detective Sergeant Lawrence O'Donnell, a 20 year veteran of the force. Known as Larry, he was a dedicated cop with a desire to keep law and order within his community as well as in his own camp, and although he closed his eyes to minor incidences within his jurisdiction, he would never tolerate any major tampering within his department.

Niki felt the coolness of the metal chair against her legs. It caused her to fidget and reposition herself. She sat alone and afraid but determined to see this through. The revolving shadows on the ceiling reminded her how hot the day was. She was tired and grateful the fan above her was working to some degree. The phone on the desk resonated non-stop. Its incessant ringing added to her uneasiness. Should she leave before someone picks it up?

"Can I help you, Ma'am?" The voice was strong and forceful.

Niki turned and found she was staring into the bluest eyes she had ever seen. "I don't know," she responded. Her answer was weak and unsure. "I hope you can."

"What seems to be the trouble, Ma'am?" The tall, stocky man

appeared impatient as he entered the room, anticipating a routine interview that would prove uneventful. Niki's hands began to shake. She felt her legs go weak. She was grateful she was still sitting.

Sensing her uneasiness, the sergeant offered her a cup of coffee. "No, thanks," Niki replied, "I had one about an hour ago. I'm going to say what I came to say and be done with it. The rest is in your hands."

He extended his hand toward Niki. "I'm Sergeant Larry O'Donnell," he grinned. "I run this place, and you are—?"

"My name is Niki Hughes," Her hand vibrated as she shook his.

"Have a seat here, Ma'am," Larry instructed, pulling a chair away from the window and taking a seat behind his desk opposite Niki. "Now what seems to be the trouble, Young Lady?"

"I would like to report some wrongdoing within your department," Niki's face was ashen.

"I have to warn you, Miss Hughes, I will be taking down your statements, so please try to be accurate. Let's start from the beginning."

After an hour and a half and two cups of coffee, forced on her by a skeptical police sergeant, Niki asked if she could leave. "My mother is waiting in the car, Sergeant. I have to be going."

"There's one more question," the sergeant said. "Your accusations are serious. Can you describe the three officers you saw in the courtyard one more time?"

"It was a parking lot—and I told you the first man was about six feet, two inches tall, hefty."

"Like me?" Larry interrupted.

"I suppose so. His hair was lighter sort of blond with grey in it," she answered. "The woman, who came after, was tall."

"How tall?"

"Oh, about five foot eleven, maybe six feet. She was in the passenger seat of the second police car. Her skin was dark, and her hair was black and shoulder length." The officer with her was of medium height about 5 ft. 8 inches with sandy brown hair."

"What it comes down to is you're accusing the Camwood Police Department of a serious crime, Miss Hughes. Drug trafficking is a felony, and if the media should get wind of this, the Governor would call for a full investigation of the department. Are you aware of the time and money that would go into this investigation? Not to mention the lives affected by it?"

"I do, Sir," Niki answered.

The sergeant had hoped Niki would slip up on some of her statements, but after interrogating her repeatedly, her testimony remained intact. He found no inconsistencies.

"I'm going to do an inside investigation of my department before I report this to my superiors, Miss Hughes. Don't go too far in case we need to talk to you again."

"Fair enough, Sergeant," Niki got up to leave.

"We have your address and phone number. We'll be in touch."

Satisfied she had performed her mission, Niki found her way to the Ladies Room. Leaning against the restroom door, she sighed deeply and began to pray. "Lord, You see all things, and You know I have done my part. Please protect us, and You be the final judge."

Splashing some cold water on her face, she composed herself and returned to her waiting mother, who by this time had stepped out of the hot car. Sarah found her seated on a bench, her facial expression unchanged.

Sergeant Larry opened the left top drawer of his desk. He pulled out a thick brown binder and threw it forcefully across the desk's wide top. "Read it," he said to his colleague Detective Robert Banks, known as Robbie to his peers, who was currently with the Narcotics Division downtown. They had been patrolling partners for several years before they were both promoted to separate units. On occasion their roles would intertwine. Larry advanced to Detective Sergeant, working closely with both the Homicide Division and the DEA Task force. He saw his new position as grueling, yet rewarding, and worth the hassle. The idea something was amiss within his camp should have shocked him. Although he wanted to dismiss Niki's accusations, he had sensed something was going down for some time. He couldn't put his finger on it. On occasion, both men would help each other out.

Robbie picked up the binder, opened it, and began to read out loud. "Larson—Anderson—Balboa...White—McNary—Deeds." His voice heightened, "You mean you have suspected these men of something all along and never led on to anyone?"

The sergeant pursed his lips, and his brow furrowed into one long line between his eyes. "Let's say I'm keeping a personal watch on them.

There is one person on my list I'm looking hard at right now. I never got around to doing a thorough check on him, but I intend to. I guess I was telling myself I needed a better reason. You know, the loyalty thing."

"You have one now." Robbie said. "Any chance you'll fill me in on who it is?"

The sound of footsteps disrupted the pair. Robbie threw the binder back at the sergeant who placed it inside his desk drawer. He turned the brass key and slid the key into his shirt pocket. Eyeing his ex-partner, he sat upright in his swivel chair as Officer Brian White appeared in the doorway. "What can I do for you, White?" he asked.

"I'm checking in before my tour starts, Sarge. Anything special you want?"

"Yeah, run down Chen Young on Pier 33, and fill me in on what he's doing. I haven't heard anything in two days.

"Ah, the boondocks." White smirked.

The sergeant continued to brief Officer White on the details of Chen's assignment, but the mistrust he had for him was real.

A cooler stood to the left of the entrance door. Walking over to it, Officer White pulled a cup from the dispenser and poured himself the cold liquid. He was sweating. Larry sensed his uneasiness. Both men watched silently as the officer turned and walked out, closing the heavy door behind him. They watched until he stepped into the elevator.

Robbie studied his counterpart's face for a few moments. "I'm going to need help on this one," Larry said. The old schoolhouse lamp on the ceiling above the desk started to flicker. The sergeant glanced upward and shook his head. "Leave maintenance a note for me on your way out. Will you, Robbie?" he instructed. "Tell them to fix this thing."

"I no longer work here, remember?" Robbie quipped. "So long Sarge, keep me posted."

~ CHAPTER SEVEN ~

"Turn that darn thing down!" Larry roared, "I can't think." Avoiding the instruction from his superior, Detective Chen Young scanned the screen in front of him with the speakers blasting. "Did you hear me, Young?" the sergeant asked.

"Sorry, Sarge. What's up?" Chen rose from his chair and walked over to the small alcove near his desk. He poured himself a cup of fresh decaf and turned to his superior. He anticipated a long list of reprimands for the past two weeks of work. He knew he had not delivered, and he dreaded the confrontation.

"What have you been doing lately, Young? You haven't given me anything."

"It's been two weeks since I started the assignment," Chen replied, "two weeks."

"Look, Chen, I may have to take you off the docks. We need surveillance right here in Camwood. We suspect something is going on within our precinct, and I need you to start tomorrow. Come to my office at 9 a.m. I'll brief you then. You're not to mention this to anyone. I'll have to get a replacement on 33."

For a split-second Chen's hands brushed across his chest as if he was shielding himself from a bullet. He turned away so Larry would not read into it. "Thanks, Sarge. I was hoping to get away from the docks. See you in the morning."

The two men met at 9 a.m. sharp. Larry still hadn't made up his mind about Chen Young. He knew if he was going to get to the bottom of things, he would have to start trusting someone. He reasoned Chen was the least likely to look for trouble since he had been with his department just a little over a year. Questionable incidences were taking place. Until Niki Hughes walked into the stationhouse, he had tried to push them away. Unaccounted time and extra spending were the minor thorns in his side. Now his mood had shifted. If corruption existed within the department, his priority was to find the ones responsible and have them prosecuted.

"Am I going to have back up with this assignment?" Chen asked. "What about Larson or Joe Balboa? I think Balboa might be available."

Larry was unaware of the relationship Chen had with Joe. He said he would consider it and get back to him. He did not mention Joe was on the top of his list of suspects; in fact, he mentioned no names at all. His briefing lasted almost one hour. "Keep your eyes and ears open and report back to me," Larry instructed. "Discuss this with no one." They shook hands and parted.

Larry's doubtful expression lingered after Chen left his office. *I don't have enough to worry about trying to keep this city under control, now everyone's a suspect?* The drive home gave him time to think. It occurred to him Niki was adamant about an Asian man being involved in the transaction she witnessed. *Could it be Chen?* Appeasing himself, his thought vanished. His mind shut down for at least 7 hours. He would continue to use Chen Young.

Facing Robbie Banks, Sergeant Larry sat in his office. "I spoke to Chen today. I have to start believing in someone if I'm going to get anywhere," he lied.

"I know," Robbie answered, "but I've got a bad feeling about this. Maybe you should have sent Deeds, or — ."

The knock on the door was forceful. "Enter," both men called out simultaneously. Larry grabbed a cigarette and sucked in a wad of smoke. He looked up as Officer Joe Balboa entered the room.

"Speak of the devil," Robbie said, unaware his words were prophetic. "I was about to mention your name."

"I hope in a good way, Banks," Joe said. He laughed.

Larry had trusted his colleague in the past; however, the description given to him of one of the officers in the parking area below Niki's window matched Joe to a T. "What brings you to this neck of the woods?" Robbie asked. Without waiting for a reply, he added, "How's the detail in Chinatown going?"

"We have a few leads," Joe looked directly at Larry. "That's why I'm here. I heard you're scouting for someone to cover the local areas. I wanted to request you keep me on my detail for a while longer. I'm getting close, and I don't want to abandon it now."

Larry eyed Joe for a few seconds. "What makes you think I'd take you off of it, Balboa?"

"Don't know exactly, but I thought I might be a contender. I'm beginning to get somewhere. I handed in my report last week. Did you read it?"

"I read it. You didn't give me enough details, only that you had a lead on the Liu gang being responsible for trafficking in the high school on the west side. I need to have more than that. There are many gangs in Chinatown, Joe. You need to give me the meat, not the milk. You can follow that one lead, but it may not pan out, and if it doesn't, you have nothing." Larry stood and walked to the window. "I need names, Joe. I want the names of the pushers. I don't give a hoot about what gang they're in."

"Give me more time, and I'll deliver. I promise."

Larry sensed Joe's uneasiness. He shot a glance at Robbie as the door closed behind him. They both stared at each other for several seconds and said nothing. "Put a tail on him."

Robbie smirked. "Consider it done."

Chen Young glanced at his watch. His pacing was interrupted by the sound of footsteps. "Sorry I'm late. I had to run an errand for my wife." Joe shook his head as he caught Chen's facial expression. "You see how foggy it is. Did you want me in one piece or not? I couldn't see two feet in front of me. Anyway, I'm here."

The mist began to encircle the two men while they stood under the streetlamp on Camwood's High Street. "Let's get started. We must come up with some evidence, or the sarge will catch on. It's not going to work much longer." Joe's tone was rigid. "You drive tonight—I'll do the talking."

Chen motioned for Joe to get in his car. He could sense the uneasiness in his friend's voice as the tan sedan pulled away from the curb. With the headlights off, he continued to drive slowly toward the docks at the edge of town. The route took them in the direction of the China District. As they got nearer, their eyes focused on a rainbow of lights peeking through the fog. Both men could hear echoes of stringed instruments as they meandered in and out of the winding alleys. "Chinatown at its best," Joe said.

Chen drove through the dark streets for another mile until Joe shouted for him to pull over to the side. He stopped the car but kept the motor running. "Do you see that guy over there—the one coming out of Dim's Bar?" Joe asked.

"Yeah."

"He was my first connection into the system. He introduced me to all the head honchos. After getting to know them, it became easy. You know what I mean. I could get the stuff whenever I wanted. No questions asked."

Chen listened but did not respond. Noticing the fog was lifting, he pulled away from the curb. As the sedan headed toward the pier, Joe filled his cohort in on their course of action for the night. "We have to target someone," he said. "The sarge expects names."

"And who are you going to turn on?" Chen asked.

"Listen. I don't have a choice. It's either me or them. For now, I'll throw him a couple of bogus names. It'll give me more time while he investigates. Then I'll make my next move."

"Which is what? He wants someone he can track down, Joe. Someone's got to be the scapegoat. Who do you have in mind?"

"A person that won't rat on us, of course. There are pigeons out there that don't know our territory but are involved enough to be prosecuted. They will sing. I can pin the trafficking on any one of these canaries without them pulling our plug."

Chen's eyes narrowed, and he shifted his position. Sensing his uncertainty, Joe explained. "They will cave, but they don't know the names of the big guys who we deal with. We'll be okay."

Chen drove slowly toward the holding dock. The headlights remained off.

Dozens of forklift trucks were lined up in neat rows in front of the storage areas. They provided a perfect retreat for Chen to park. He turned to Joe and offered him a cigarette which his friend gratefully took. They remained in the area for some time. Joe briefed Chen on a few names he intended to give the sergeant in the morning. The smell of the river enveloped the two men. Chen rolled up the window. "We'd better get going. It must be low tide."

~ CHAPTER EIGHT ~

Neva Pelleron's plane touched down at the San Juan International Airport, much later than its intended arrival. Although Neva was on in years, she had never felt as old as this night. *Maybe I shouldn't have stayed so long in Camwood,* she thought. However, the experience of meeting Niki and Sarah planted a sweet memory in her mind which she had doted on throughout the flight.

Neva rose from her seat and welcomed the helping hand of the stranger who sat behind her. He attempted to retrieve her overnight case resting in the cubicle above. "I'll get that for you, Ma'am," the tall southerner proclaimed in a husky voice. He stretched out his massive arms and handed her the oblong case.

"Why thank you, Young Man." She smiled. "God bless you." What's your name if you don't mind my asking?"

The man returned her smile, revealing a set of yellow, rotting teeth. "Tom Black's the name, Ma'am—but all my friends call me Tex." He tipped his wide cowboy hat. "Where are you heading when you get off this old machine? May I ask?"

"Oh, I'm not too far from this airport, only a few miles." Neva said. "I live near Ocean Park. I have lived there most of my married life, and I have remained there after my husband passed away."

"Now isn't that a coincidence. I'm going that way myself. Mind if we share a cab?" Knowing she would not need to waste time finding a porter, Neva gladly accepted the invitation.

The taxi pulled up to Neva's front entrance at dusk. The pure white stucco walls and red tiled roof stood out among the other houses in the twilight, keeping to the tradition of the ancient city several miles to the west of her. It was a tranquil place, dotted with almond trees that shaded the small villa, while catching the sea breezes on a summer night.

Neva was proud of her home, built in the early 1930's. Its proximity to the seaside and the Caribbean drew her to the area. She was well known at several of the posh hotels and often stayed as a guest, compliments of the staff, for sending many tourists their way. She enjoyed sitting in the courtyards that overlooked the white sand beaches. She would gaze out over the lagoon to watch the kayaks and small boats glide by. She felt blessed for her eighty odd years on the earth, and grateful she was still healthy enough to savor each day she was given.

Tex had been less talkative in the taxi. As the cab stopped along the curbside, he jumped out. "Let me take your bags in for you, Ma'am."

Before she could reply, he lifted the two large bags and the oblong overnight case from the trunk of the taxi and dropped them onto the ground. Following Neva to her front porch, he thanked her for the pleasant company, and as she requested, he left her luggage on the doorstep. He bade her goodbye, walked to the taxi and turned abruptly. "Would you mind if I called on you sometime, Ma'am? You see, I'm a stranger to this area, here on business, and I don't know anyone. It can get lonely."

Neva's smile was faint. She knew exactly what he was talking about. "You're welcome anytime, Mr. Black. You have my number now. I'll look forward to hearing from you soon."

Neva hesitated at the door long enough to watch the tall Texan be whisked away. After bringing her luggage into the vestibule, she closed the door, fastened its bolts, and walked over to the living room sofa. It was there she succumbed to her weariness and fell into a deep sleep.

Several hours passed before Neva heard the clock in the hallway chime. "Oh, my Lord," she said, "I've slept half the night already." Finding her way to the bedroom, she washed up and placed her dental plates in a cup of fizzling cleanser. For the second time, she collapsed, grateful it was on her huge pine bed and remained there until the morning.

Tex had instructed the driver to take him to lodging nearest to Neva's home. He arrived at the motel fifteen minutes later. He showered and shaved, dressed casually for dinner, and returned shortly after 10 p.m. He threw himself across the bed and picked up the phone on the nightstand. "Operator, get me long distance." He began to tap on the local directory with his pen. He tapped until he heard the voice on the other end of the line.

"Hello, who is this?"

Tex could barely hear who was speaking. "Is that you, Joe? I can hardly hear you," he hollered.

"Yeah, it's me—that you, Tex?"

Tex laughed. "It's me alright. This is going to be easier than I thought—a piece of cake." They talked for about ten minutes. As the conversation ended, Tex said, "I'll be in touch." He laughed again.

Joe listened to the laughter until it melted into static, and he could hear no more. He hung up satisfied.

~ CHAPTER NINE ~

Anne Terrance beamed as she watched Jack and Sean exit the train at the Amtrak Station. Not expecting her, they walked toward the exit gates. Choosing to take the stairs, than wait for the elevator, they entered the crowded station's main area and passed swiftly by Anne who had been watching from the window above. Unheeding her repetitive calls, they approached the ticket counter located in the middle of the room. Jack reached into his pocket and retrieved his wallet. Hoping to secure a taxi ride home, he was interrupted by a high-pitched voice calling out to him. As he turned and gazed over his shoulder, he spotted his future fiancée running toward him.

"Hey, Girl," he shouted as he picked Anne up and swung her around. "Sean, look who's here." He held Anne in his arms. Looking bored, Sean gazed upward, uninterested in the means used to get from the terminal to his front door. It wasn't that Sean was jealous of Anne's relationship with his father; in fact, he kind of liked her and often bragged to his friends about her good looks. But now he was tired and hungry. It was as simple as that.

"I parked in lot B," Anne said. "Come on. You guys must be exhausted. Let's get out of here."

As Anne pulled out of the parking lot, she was unaware of the black Chevy sedan following close behind. There was no end to their conversation during the forty-five minute drive to Jack's home. Sean was passed out in the back seat. After hearing a few short snorts, they both chuckled when they saw Sean's mouth wide open and his head hanging over the edge.

Turning into the driveway, Anne pulled up to the garage and turned off the ignition. She leaned over and kissed Jack. She hoped Sean was still asleep. After exchanging some words and nudging Sean, Jack gathered his belongings along with his son's and bid her farewell. He promised he would call her first thing in the morning.

Anne had made plans to see her mother that evening. After watching Jack and Sean disappear into the house, she backed out of the driveway and hung a left, heading toward town. She continued to drive in the opposite direction of her home. Passing by the northeast corner of the street, she noticed a black sedan in her rear view mirror. She didn't give it a second thought.

~ CHAPTER TEN ~

Marge Bernside could not take her eyes off the heart monitor. Listening to its consistent rhythm assured her that her husband was in good hands. She knew Harry well enough to assume his attack was brought on by stress, rather than anything else. She also knew there was one person who would be able to fill in the gaps of what may have triggered his heart attack. Aware it was nearing 11 p.m. and a new shift would be arriving, she lifted the receiver of the bedside phone and was interrupted by two nurses who had come on duty.

"Hello, Mrs. Bernside, how are you holding up?" asked the tall, dark haired woman. She looked at least forty and walked with a slight limp. She was followed by a petite woman, her blond hair pulled back in a tight bun. She appeared to be in her thirties.

Marge placed the receiver back in its cradle and looked up. Uninterested, the younger nurse brushed past her. Marge's smile was half-hearted, she was too tired to respond. The two nurses approached the bed and proceeded to turn down the side rails. "What are you doing?" Marge asked, "He's sleeping soundly."

"We won't be a minute, Mrs. Bernside. "We want to reposition him," the dark-haired nurse explained. Marge thought they were being insensitive and was relieved when they departed and left her in solitude.

She picked up the receiver and began to dial an outside line.

Farley Chisom was one of the respected members on the board at Filtrec Electroics Corp. He had been Harry's colleague for twenty years. They worked together on several major projects the company had delved into, the most recent one being presented to the board by Harry. At least that was his intention. Farley was unaware that Harry's presentation did not go off as planned.

Marge wondered why Farley wasn't picking up the phone. It was after eleven and not like him to have retired early. After the usual, "We can't come to the phone right now," she slammed the receiver down. "Oh, how I hate these things," she said aloud, refusing to identify herself. She walked close to Harry's bedside and leaned over and kissed him on the forehead. It was sweaty and cool. Had he developed a fever earlier in the evening that had broken? Marge pressed the call button and waited for at least five minutes before the nurse with the limp came to the door.

"Can I help you, Mrs. Bernside?"

"I was wondering if my husband had a temperature today?"

"No, he didn't. All his vital signs were stable," she smiled. "I wouldn't worry myself. Why don't you go home and get some rest. You've had a long day."

Returning to his bedside, Marge wiped Harry's forehead with a cool washcloth and straightened out his blankets. Hesitant to leave, she turned for one last look at her husband and exited the room that would become familiar to her the next few days. She made a brief stop at the Nurses Station before entering the elevator. "Call me at any hour if you need me," she instructed the nurse at the desk.

Marge couldn't get the key into the door lock fast enough to reach the phone. Thinking it might be Farley, she raced into the living room and grabbed the receiver. It was too late; whoever it was had hung up. Reaching into her purse, she pulled out her address book and dialed Farley's number. She was relieved when she heard the husky voice on the other end. "Hello, Farley, it's Marge" she said, "I tried to get you earlier. Am I calling too late?"

"No, not at all, I just returned from California," he responded. "You know how things are with the firm, one day here—one day there."

Marge began to give Farley an account of what took place that day.

"I was hoping you could give me some insight into what could have triggered his heart attack. He's been so uptight about the job lately, but I never expected it would come to this." Her tone was somber.

"I've been away for two weeks, Marge. I only got a chance to speak to Harry once. The last time we spoke he was okay. We talked about the presentation he was to give to the board members, and he seemed pumped up about it. He was looking forward to going over his ideas with me when I returned from California."

The conversation lasted a minute more, and after thanking Farley for his time, Marge went straight into the den and opened the secretary where Harry kept a duplicate set of keys. Holding the large metal ring, which carried about ten keys of different sizes, she fingered her way through them until she felt the ones she knew to be the master keys to his office and desk. Pulling them off the ring, she carefully placed them in her handbag. "Tomorrow I'll find out what's going on," she said. "If no one will help me, I'm going to help myself."

~ CHAPTER ELEVEN ~

Officer Brian White sat in his favorite chair. Looking forward to catching a double header on TV, he rested his feet on the glass topped coffee table. Annoyed he had forgotten to pick up an extra pack of cigarettes from the local deli, he poured himself a cold beer and settled in.

Brian and Joe Balboa had spent many years as a team, combing the streets of Camwood on the graveyard shift, until Joe was given a new partner. They had lost touch with each other except for a brief meeting now and then at the station house—until recently.

Life was good, Brian thought. He had been divorced for ten years. His wife, being an account executive, hadn't demanded much. This allowed him the resources to invest in his children's education. His son Brian, Jr. was completing his final year at a college in the South. His daughter Lucille was a graduate of a school of design in New York City and trying her best to break into the competitive world of fashion. Deep in thought, he did not hear the phone ring until the caller rang a second time. Brian jumped up, mumbling under his breath and hurried into the living room. He picked up the receiver as the caller was about to hang up.

"Hello, Brian, are you there?"

"I'm here. Who's this?"

"It's me, Joe."

"Joe, did you have to call now? I'm about to watch a game."

"Listen, Brian. We have to talk. It's important."

"Ok, make it quick. What's up?"

"I'll get right to the point. Someone witnessed the transaction between me and Chen Young that night in the parking lot. It was reported to the sarge, and now the whole department is under investigation." His voice got louder as he spoke, "and, if they saw me and Chen, they also saw you and Maddie."

"Are you sure about this? How'd you find out?"

"It leaked out somehow, and anyone that's breathing is under suspicion, even the meter maids."

"You went into the B&B. You saw and heard nothing. You said so yourself."

"I know, but because the place was quiet it doesn't mean everyone was asleep. Someone reported it. How else would the sarge have found out?"

"You're over thinking it," Brian replied. "Stop worrying until you have a real reason to worry. No one has been ID'd. Now can I get back to my game?"

"I'm not finished. You are as involved as I am. On the way out I clipped the sign in book on a table in the hallway. It has the signature of all the guests staying there that week. We must find out who reported us. If they can identify us, we are all going under, and that's you included. I have Chen working on it as we speak. I'm going to need your help. I'll call you in a few days and fill you in on the details. You'd better be around. Enjoy your game."

Brian sank to the floor. His look was anemic. He must have sat there for at least ten minutes before he attempted to pull himself up. He returned to the den and took the beer he had left on the coffee table and threw it across the room; the projectile hit the fireplace mantle. Shards of glass flew in every direction; most of them landing on the tiled hearth. Returning to his chair, he collapsed. His expression was stoic as he gazed at the deer head mounted on the wall above the fireplace. He had often bragged about the trophy to his buddies at the station. Suddenly it didn't seem important anymore. "I've got to figure this thing out," he said aloud. "The fingers can't point to me. If they do, I'm finished."

~ CHAPTER TWELVE ~

The plane touched down at Heathrow Airport shortly after 3 p.m. As the wheels of the jetliner touched the runway, Niki and Sarah heaved a sigh of relief. It had drizzled most of the afternoon, and the sky remained dark. After picking up their luggage, the two women hailed a taxi and hoped they would reach their hotel before the predicted second shower broke through the clouds. They were grateful when they arrived at their hotel in a little under an hour, despite the traffic, thanks to a young London cabbie. He was anxious to call it a day.

A doorman in a dark suit, his outfit complete with a white bow tie and black derby hat, ushered the ladies through the massive brass and glass door. Niki's large eyes widened as she canvassed the Lobby. "I feel pampered already, Mom," she said. "Thanks so much for this trip. I needed it—we both needed it."

"It's the least I can do," Sarah said. "You were so stressed out after our Camwood trip. You deserved a break—even more than I did. It's English hospitality. Get used to it."

The concierge greeted the two women as they approached the main desk. "We've been expecting you, Ladies. Welcome to St. Simeon's." His voice was refined. Niki studied the long thin features of his face and decided he had not been a concierge all his adult life but a commodore in the Royal Air Force. A 'what was he before this?' game she played often.

"My name is Horace Peabody. If you have any questions, please feel free to ask." He began to fill them in on everything the hotel had to offer, and handed Niki a brochure, complete with pictures, pool and spa schedules, and menus which included all meals along with Dining Room and Pub hours. "Don't forget to visit our Fitness Center," he added.

Niki was impressed. "Englishmen. Would you expect less?" she whispered to Sarah. They both laughed.

After checking in, the ladies ascended the marble staircases that merged onto the second floor. Niki took the left stairs and Sarah the right. The staircases were adorned with shiny brass banisters that captured their reflections as they found their way to the next level.

"We could have taken the elevator," Sarah remarked, puffing a little as she reached the second floor.

"I know, Mom. I wanted to make a grand entrance." "Sorry."

Their room was located at the end of a long corridor. As the bellhop escorted them, the ladies shoes sunk deep into the plush carpeting. It wasn't the normal flat floor covering you would see in a motel or cheap guesthouse. It was the palatial kind that made them want to take their shoes off and walk barefoot. They looked at each other and smiled.

"The bellhop unlocked the door and handed them the keys. He bowed slightly, "The rest of your luggage will be up in a moment. Enjoy your stay."

"Thank you. I'm sure we will," Niki placed a generous tip in his hand.

After several minutes the remainder of their luggage arrived. They decided not to unpack, except for their pj's, robes, and toiletries, and to spend the evening in their room.

The room was spacious with creamy vanilla walls and thick moldings. The large windows carried heavy cobalt blue drapery that was topped with a floral canopy of English Chintz. Two fireside chairs of a burnt orange print flanked a white marble fireplace which was centered between oak bookcases. Each one held a complete library of books. The pair changed their clothes and curled up into the chairs. They both chose books on English history. "Mom, this couldn't be lovelier," Niki commented. They read for the remainder of the afternoon.

It was nearly 6 p.m. when Room Service arrived with their dinner. Wanting to have a traditional English supper, Sarah chose the roast beef with mashed potatoes, and Niki enjoyed leg of baby lamb, sautéed spinach, and charcoal roasted yams. Their dinner was followed by desserts of sweet syrup pudding and a rhubarb custard tart that they both shared.

"Mom, what are your plans for tomorrow?" Niki asked.

"How about visiting a London flea market?" I think we should act like tourists and see the usual attractions. I hear that Camden Market is the best one; they have everything from jewelry and clothing to antiques, so why don't we check it out?"

Niki agreed. "You're the tourist guide. It sounds great."

The ladies rose early the next morning and enjoyed a breakfast in the hotel dining room, consisting of honey baked ham and eggs for Sarah and a continental breakfast of homemade croissants with fresh marmalade for Niki. The waiter gave each woman a small china pot of brewed English coffee. They considered it the highlight of the morning. As Sarah took her first sip, a thought entered her mind. "Niki, did you have to get permission from the sergeant in Camwood to leave the country? It never occurred to me to ask. Didn't he tell you not to go too far?"

"You know, Mom, you're right. I never gave it a thought. I'll get in touch with him while we are away and let him know, in case he needs to contact us."

They arrived at Camden Stables market a few minutes after 10 a.m. and were eager to visit the many fashion stalls, which offered a variety of dresses, skirts, and belts, with a special eye out for vintage clothing. As they were breezing through the narrow alleys of the market, Sarah caught sight of a full length skirt of embroidered cotton. She picked it up and lifted it to her face. "Feel how soft this is, Niki." She gently caressed her cheek with the garment. "It reminds me of Tante Anna."

"Who's that?" Niki's eyes narrowed.

"Tante Anna was a sweet old Italian woman who influenced my childhood back in the day," she answered. "All the neighbors loved her, and she loved everyone in return. If she favored you, you were sure to get one of her treasures as a gift. She would embroider her own designs onto a blouse or skirt and find a reason to give each away. If you didn't have a special occasion, she would invent one, and before long you would receive one of her masterpieces."

"Why didn't you ever tell me about her?" Niki asked.

"Sometimes your mind needs a boost, something to trigger your memory, and the embroidered skirt did it for me."

As the Women walked through the narrow passageways, Sarah reminisced about one of these happier times. "I remember receiving one of her creations—it was my birthday. Tante brought me the most beautiful white blouse I had ever seen. I must have been about eight years old." Her smile broadened. "It had red and yellow flowers hand stitched onto the blouse and puffy short sleeves with small ruffled edges. I loved that blouse so much I wore it to school several days in a row, not caring what anyone thought. I was determined to wear it as often as I could. Whenever I see fancy stitching on a garment, I think of Tante Anna, and how special she made me feel."

Returning to the moment, Sarah asked, "Are you going to go back and buy that shawl you saw?"

"That was an hour ago, it must be sold by now."

Sarah turned and grabbed Niki's hand, and with a twinkle in her eye, she escorted her back to the rack of shawls. "It's the gold one over there with the fringe Isn't it?"

Niki laughed. "Yes, that's the one."

"It's yours now."

The marketplace was unusually crowded for a weekday. The voices of the merchants barking at the tourists to buy their wares could be heard from all directions. You could barely hear the church bells echoing in the distance.

After making the purchase for her daughter, the two women decided to stop at a stall of hanging belts. Niki had been looking for a patent leather belt since the beginning of the summer and thought she would find it in Camden. Sarah was lagging behind a bit and stopped at a rack of dresses about twenty five feet from her daughter. Niki reached her destination, a small booth at the end of the alley. The perfect belt caught her eye. Holding it up, Niki yelled across the rows of hanging dresses that were separating her from her mother. "Look, Mom," she cried out, as she raised her trophy. She dropped her wallet as she spoke.

Sarah witnessed the blunder and yelled back, "Be careful, hurry, grab it."

Heeding her mother's warning, Niki bent down to grab the wallet but lost sight of it as the shoppers rushed by, flanking her on either side. It was only when she felt a hand on her shoulder and heard the reassuring words, "Is this what you are looking for?" did she find peace.

"Why, yes," Niki smiled a wide and grateful smile. "It's mine."

As she rose from the ground, Niki found herself staring into the warm, friendly, eyes of her good Samaritan. "With all these people around, how did you ever notice what happened?"

"Oh, I'm known for my observations," the short dark-haired man answered. "They call me "Laser" for my sharp eyes." His smile was comforting. They both laughed.

The man held out his hand. Niki reciprocated and thanked him. "Are you visiting relatives here in London or a tourist like myself?" he asked.

"Guilty of the latter."

"Where are you staying?"

Not wanting to get too familiar with her new acquaintance, she skirted around the question. "Oh, we're a few miles from here."

"I'm staying at the Colony. I'm not with a tour. It can get lonesome at times. Maybe we can have lunch sometime. How long will you be staying abroad?"

Before Niki could answer the gentleman, Sarah approached them. "Mom, this nice man found my wallet—wait a minute," Niki turned to her hero, "I don't even know your name."

"My name is Chen Young. At your service, Miss."

"Meet Chen Young," Niki turned to her mother. "We owe him one. Don't you agree? Maybe we should invite him to dinner one evening." Without waiting for her mother's approval, Niki turned to Chen. "How long do you expect to be in London?"

"Around two weeks."

"That gives us plenty of time." Niki shot a glance at Sarah.

"Of course, we'd be happy to have you join us for dinner, Mr. Young."

"Please call me Chen."

Sarah left the details up to her daughter and continued shopping. Niki was skeptical about giving Chen the location of her hotel. She opened her handbag and retrieved a pen. Ripping off a portion of an old envelope, she jotted down her phone number and handed it to her new acquaintance. "You can call me whenever your schedule allows, and we'll meet for dinner somewhere in town. My mother and I will choose a decent place. I promise." They both laughed.

Niki's eyes followed Chen's disappearance into the crowd. She was grateful for his act of valor, but her instinct told her to tread lightly. A dinner and small talk would suffice for his kindness.

The soft velvet peals of familiar chimes, coming from the old church tower in Camden Town, interweaved the narrow passages, finding their way through the marketplace. As the hammer struck the huge brass and metal bell, its muffled sounds reminded Niki it was two o'clock.

Sarah, who had continued her hunt for a bargain, heard her daughter's voice call out over the bins of shoes and bags.

"Let's grab some lunch. I'm starving," Niki yelled.

"Good Idea," Sarah agreed. "Looks like rain," she looked skyward.

"Good old English rain." Niki laughed. "I'll flag a taxi."

The raindrops hit the window of the cab as soon as the two women stepped into it. Niki didn't speak a word during the ride to the hotel. A thought kept nudging her. *I think I've seen him before*. She decided not to say anything to her mother, at least not for the time being.

Declining any offers he received from the cabbies prowling about, Chen Young walked back to his hotel. He had heard stories before about how some taxi drivers take advantage of American tourists. He decided not to be a statistic. During his stay in London, he would walk as much as possible. As he walked, passersby could hear him mumbling the word, "bingo!"

~ CHAPTER THIRTEEN ~

Brushing a piece of lint off his shirt, Tex stepped out of the taxi in front of Neva's home. He could feel the beads of perspiration begin to form on his forehead. He pulled out a clean handkerchief from his back pocket and wiped his forehead. He approached the entrance door and pressed hard on the bell. *What a way to make a buck, dragging around an old broad.* On second thought he relished how profitable it would be if Neva was the one they were looking for. *Keep telling yourself you'll be home in two weeks, Tommy Boy.* He began to smile the same crooked smile he always had when he was about to pull the wool over someone's eyes.

The door swung open to reveal the lovely face of the woman he had met only a few days earlier. Neva looked smart with her hair pinned back, two flowered pins holding it in place. She had added a slight peach blush to her rounded cheeks and a dab of coral lipstick to her thin lips. She couldn't remember when she had last worn lipstick, but after considering it she decided, "Why not."

"You look lovely," Tex said politely. "Are you ready for a night on the town?" Not taking the compliment to heart, Neva chuckled. A tropical shower had cooled things off earlier in the day. She had reminded herself to bring her lace shawl in case the restaurant was too cold, not that it would have done much good. She grabbed it on her way out.

As twilight spread its rays over the horizon, the pair exchanged small talk. Darkness fell as soon as the cab pulled up to the small cafe at the north edge of the city.

In his younger days Tex had visited the island often as a go between for a drug kingpin who worked the beach clubs. He was hoping he wouldn't run into any of his old friends with Neva in tow. The maitre d' greeted them and ushered them to a table in the back of the cafe.

"Would you like a cocktail to start, Mrs. P? You don't mind if I call you Mrs. P. do you?"

Tex pulled out Neva's chair and placed her shawl around her shoulders. She felt pampered.

"As to your first question, yes, I would love a cocktail, and as to your second question, you may call me anything that makes you comfortable. I would appreciate it if you would order for me. Tonight, I would like to live dangerously."

"I'd be delighted. Please call me Tex," he exposed his eroding teeth.

"Why am I not surprised that people call you Tex?" Neva opened her napkin and placed it on her lap.

Tex grinned. He was annoyed the dinner took up most of the evening. He was glad to be back in his motel room before the thunderstorm warnings became a reality. He stepped into a steamy shower and thought back to the evening's conversation. Wanting to gain Neva's trust, he had kept the conversation light. He didn't want to spend another night with the 'old woman', so he began grilling her during dessert.

"I've traveled all over the United States this year, Mrs. P," he lied. "Have you traveled much?"

Neva ignored the question. "They must keep you busy, Tex. What do you do for a living?"

Trying not to show his annoyance, he questioned her again. "Have you traveled much, Mrs. P?"

"I've been to several countries and through many of the States, most recently to the town of Camwood. Did you ever hear of it?"

"No, I haven't. Please tell me about it."

"It's a college town. It's located near a river close to a university." Her powder blue eyes twinkled as she described her favorite place. "I like college towns. Being around the youth of America—they keep you on your toes." Her laugh resonated and caught the attention of some patrons." There's a lot of culture in these small college towns. I enjoy visiting the museums and art galleries and seeing live theatre."

Hoping for a clue, Tex persisted in his interrogation. "Anything exciting happen there? I mean anything you would write about in your journal?"

"Oh, no, nothing like that. The only exciting thing is Adelaide, the proprietor of the inn I stay at, changed the breakfast menu." She chuckled.

"Go on. Tell me more."

"I did meet some lovely folks." She thought hard for a moment. "Let's see. There was a man and his son, a single mother and her daughter, and oh, a couple that acted as if it was torture to be there." Her expression changed to a frown. "However, I did feel a bit sorry for them."

Before the conversation ended, Tex knew Neva was not the person Joe Balboa was looking for. Disappointed, he abruptly changed the subject. He was relieved that she had no longer questioned his occupation. He arranged for a taxi ride back to her home.

Tex stepped out of the shower. He reached for the phone and placed a long-distance call to Camwood. "Balboa, is that you?" The static was unbearable.

"Yea, who's this?"

"It's Tex." He paused for a moment to allow the static to die down. "You're barking up the wrong palm tree, man. I'm telling you the lady is empty. I'm out of here."

Irritated that Tex would give up so easily, Joe returned the shout. His words were slow and precise. "You took her out for one night. It's not enough. You have to go back. Check out her house. See if you can find any phone records that would tie her to the Camwood Police Department. I'm warning you, if you leave now, there's nothing in it for you. That ten-gallon hat you're wearing will be the last one you'll ever buy. Give it one more shot." He didn't wait for him to respond. All Tex heard on the other end was the static.

The Puerto Rican sun beat down onto the worn bricks that lined the entranceway to Neva's garden. She reached into her apron pocket and pulled out the handkerchief she kept tucked away. She patted her brow and soaked up the beads of liquid that took residence on her forehead. "You could fry bacon on these bricks," she mumbled. Trying to create a small crevice, she pressed the hand shovel into the hard earth and began to move it back and forth. After several tries, she placed the shovel on the ground. She was breathless. "I'll never get those seeds in the ground," she panted, "I don't seem to have the strength. The rain wasn't enough to soften the dirt in this heat."

Neva was proud of her garden. Tending to it became part of her daily routine. She was especially proud of her baby orchids and her gladiolas but took the most pride in her roses of several varieties and kept them separate from the other flowers.

Feeling helpless, she conceded. She decided to wait for a good rainfall. In her attempt to rise, she fell backwards onto the ground and hit her head on one of the stones that edged her garden.

Neva's phone kept ringing. "Darn it," Tex muttered, knocking over his coffee cup as he slammed the receiver down. Hot coffee spilled onto the hard, blue carpet and splashed his polished leather shoes, staining them in long narrow streaks. "Just what I needed," he growled. He grabbed the wet towel hanging off the edge of the bed and began rubbing the tips of his shoes to try to retrieve their original shine." Why didn't she answer? Where's the old girl going to go in this heat? I'll take a run over and see what's going on."

It was around 2:30 p.m. when the taxi pulled up to the white structure. Leaving the passenger door opened, Tex jumped out of the cab and in three long strides reached the steps of Neva's home. The frustrated cabbie exited the taxi, circled it, and slammed the door shut. He mumbled curses under his breath. Without waiting for further instructions, he took off.

Getting no answer to his incessant ringing, Tex let go of the doorbell, circled the stucco building, and passed a row of bushes that hugged its side. At first glance, he failed to see the large figure crumpled in a fetal position on the ground. It took a few seconds to spot her helpless body. His lips tightened. The corners of his mouth went up in a devilish grin. "Well, well, lookie here," he said. "She saved me the trouble. The old girl saved me the trouble."

Tex proceeded onto the back porch. The screen door was unlocked, and he was able to enter the house. Without a backward glance, he found his way through the kitchen and dining area, and turned left into the hallway that led to Neva's bedroom. With the precision of a surveillance camera, his eyes circled her room. It revealed the personality of the woman who so graciously took him into her life.

Neva was disciplined in every way. As his eyes spanned the room, Tex knew he would have to leave it exactly as he had found it. He walked over to the window which faced the yard and glanced through the metal slats of the blind. He made sure the figure within his eye range was still unconscious. Satisfied, he proceeded to search the room, but felt the presence of someone other than Neva nearby. His plaid shirt cleaved to his chest. He opened the top drawer of the old oak dresser which stood against the wall. He fumbled around and glanced at himself in its mirror. The image staring back at him reminded him he was not so tough after all.

Tex continued to search the room. He removed the double mattress from the stately four poster bed, and after finding nothing he placed it back on its frame. He adjusted the sheets and pressed out the creases on the bedspread with his hands. He opened the closet located on the north wall and saw it was neatly arranged with Neva's clothing hanging on two rods. The plastic hangers were color coordinated to each garment; her shoes were placed neatly on the floor. The shelf of the closet held several phone books, a few picture albums, and two large manila folders. Tex grabbed the folders and threw them onto Neva's bed. He sat and opened each one carefully. One contained important personal papers, the other included the deed to her home, the title to her car, and her medical history. Finding nothing of value to him, he returned the folders as neatly as he had found them. He was about to close the closet door when he eyed a grey box about two feet long in the left corner of the floor. Sliding it out, he sat near the bed and opened the box. It had a label which Neva had marked, OLD BILLS, and it was sectioned off by dates. One of the sections was marked, TELEPHONE RECEIPTS. Tex smiled. *Maybe Joe was right after all.*

Tex sat there for at least half an hour and scanned through all the receipts dated during and after Neva's trip to Camwood. He found nothing. "That's it. I'm done." He walked over to the phone resting on the nightstand and dialed for a taxi dispatcher to send someone "pronto." Confident he had left the room in the condition it was found, he took one more look through the bedroom window. Neva was lying in the same position on the hard dirt. Tex half smiled and exited out the front door of the house. He stepped into the waiting cab. He requested the driver take him directly to his motel. He couldn't have cared less.

~ CHAPTER FOURTEEN ~

Jack decided to close his photography studio early. The day was crisp and cool, and he wanted to take advantage of it. He contemplated giving Anne a call to suggest a ride through the country vineyards with lunch at a seaside restaurant. It was nearing noon. Sean had asked his father to pick him up after soccer practice around six o'clock, which gave him plenty of time to spend the afternoon with his girlfriend. As he reached for the phone, it rang and startled him. "Hello, I was about to call you, Anne—funny you were thinking of me at the same time. How are you?"

"I'm fine, Jack. I haven't heard from you in a few days. I was beginning to worry."

"Are you up to a scenic ride and a fancy lunch since it's Teacher's Conference Day. You're not tied down all afternoon, are you?"

Anne hesitated for a moment, "That's why I was calling, Jack. We need to talk. I am finished at school, and yes, I would like that ride."

Jack felt a bit awkward as he sat across from Anne at lunch. He sensed something was wrong when he had spoken to her earlier, yet he thought the ride through the wine country had smoothed things over a bit. "You said we needed to talk." He raised his eyebrows. He leaned forward to listen.

Anne's tone was soft but firm. "It's been over a year since we began a relationship together, and I think it's time to talk about where this is going." She swallowed hard, "I understand how important it is for Sean to have a strong bond with you. I get that, but I want one too. There are times I don't hear from you for days, and I want an answer as to where we stand." Her voice began to quiver. She picked up her water glass and took a sip. "Be honest with me. If you want to stop seeing me for a while and get your thoughts together, I'm fine with that."

Jack sat there stunned at the suggestion they part at all. Anne had no way of knowing his plans for their future. He hadn't even so much as hinted to her that their relationship could lead to marriage. He had made up his mind in Camwood, when he had time to reflect. He would ask Anne to marry him. Now, he wished he had done it sooner. He looked at her face and saw how beautiful she was. He knew how patient she had been. He took her hand and said nothing for a moment. He pulled out a small, black leather box from his suit jacket and placed it in her hand. Stunned, she was speechless. It took several moments for Anne to compose herself. Her eyes became liquid. She held the box tightly and caressed its top with her fingers.

Anne hadn't taken notice of her surroundings when she arrived at the Blue Orchid Restaurant, nor did she hear the music piped in through the speakers that were placed throughout the room, at least not until now. Her mind became a shutter, snapping one image after another. For the first time she saw the fine white china plates trimmed in gold along with the starched cloth napkins, and she watched intently as the waiter, wearing a white jacket, poured pristine liquid into her crystal goblet. The vivid colors of the room now presented themselves to her, and as she observed the deep tones of red, teal and gold, she opened the small box. She knew this afternoon would be imbedded into her memory forever.

~ CHAPTER FIFTEEN ~

Brian White walked into the Milltown Lanes with an open mind. He anticipated meeting Sean Heaton on the first day of his assignment. He had spent the last few days researching the schools in the Milltown area. Finding Sean's name in the local paper was the stroke of luck he had hoped for. As Sean excelled in several sports, it didn't take long before he was deemed a hero for having led his soccer team to victory. He was photographed along with his team in the Milltown School Paper. The last season's news article made it to the local Towne Crier. A short visit to the library brought the information Brian was seeking, and now his plan could be put in motion.

Brian didn't like sports much. He had tried out for the baseball team in high school but never made it. By not being able to join his buddies in the game, he had lost interest in most sports, except for bowling and fishing. As he entered the bowling alley, a twinge of nostalgia caused him to stop. His mind drifted back to the small upstate town he grew up in. The only offering for the town's sparse population was the old post office which had been converted into the Dell Pine Lanes. He could almost taste the greasy fries and hear the loud rock 'n' roll music playing from the stately juke box in the corner of the cafe, always there, always available, as if it were some kind of mascot.

Brian smiled. Although his "hick town," as he called it, could not produce a version of the state-of-the-art facility he had walked into, the sounds and the smells were the same. Instead of ten alleys, his eyes spanned a room that held at least 50 lanes, all parallel to each other, all on one side of the building. The opposite side housed two hundred lockers and bathroom facilities with a full staff. Instead of the hardwood maple lanes and the old wooden balls of the past, the sound of the heavy resin and urethane balls, hitting the pins as they glided down the smooth as glass alleys, still excited him.

Brian's smile broadened when he entered the Vinyl Rainbow Grill, an eatery dubbed for the short-lived colored vinyl records put out by RCA back in the late 40's to early 50's. Its theme was mid-century with blue and pink leather booths and plenty of chrome accessories, including a miniature juke box at each table. A Rock 'n' Roll song could be heard playing in the background. The hostess approached him, wearing a blue turtleneck sweater, complete with red neck scarf, and a flair skirt with a crinoline underneath. "We have a table for one in the back of the room if you don't mind," she offered.

"That'll be fine," Brian responded. Once seated, he began to survey the walls. Two of them were covered in shadow box frames. Each frame housed a 45 RPM recording of a famous mid-century artist. He was able to read the record label on the discs closest to him, THE PLATTERS. That's as far as he got. He leaned back, placed his hands behind his head and said aloud, "Maybe I'm home after all." Several heads turned. He ignored them.

A friendly tone interrupted Brian's visions of happier times. "What will it be, Sir?"

"What's the best you've got?" He did not bother to look through the menu placed between the salt and pepper shakers.

"For you, how about a nice sirloin steak with homemade garlic mashed potatoes and gravy?" she quipped.

"You're kidding, right?" He noticed the smug look on her face. "How about the house special? What might that be?"

"Two dogs and house fries with a soda of your choice."

"If it's the best you can do, okay."

"Be out in a minute," she hurried off to the kitchen.

"No rush," he yelled back with a hint of sarcasm. "I've nothing better to do."

It took no longer than ten minutes before his lunch was placed before him. Once again, the smell of the greasy fries brought back the memory of his high school days. He ate with gusto.

"How's it going?" a waitress asked as she passed by his table.

"Fine, just fine," Brian responded.

"Good," her eyes pointed toward the entrance door, "because here come the troops."

"By the troops, I gather you mean the kids are out of school now?" Before she could answer, a stampede of teens rushed through the door and nearly knocked over one of the staff.

"You've got that right," she disappeared into the kitchen.

This was the moment Brian had been waiting for. He decided he would ask as little questions of the staff as possible. He did not want to draw attention to himself and thought if he sat and listened, he may hear Sean's name come up in conversation, or better yet, get to meet him. Ordering dessert and coffee allowed him to linger unnoticed.

The first group of summer students was boisterous and rude. They ordered the waitress to bring the usual. The second group was polite. The only objection Brian had was when the youngest looking student pulled out a pack of cigarettes and a lighter and lit up."He looks like he belongs in grammar school," he mumbled. Even being a crooked cop did not nullify his fatherly instincts. The last group piled in one booth like sardines, and Brian considered it luck he was able to hear most of their conversation. He learned they were seniors, the same school year Sean was in. *If he's not here, I'll have to find out what days his team bowls and become a regular customer for awhile.* He had it all planned out. Sipping his coffee, he would wait for the right person to lead him to Sean.

"Want more coffee?" his waitress approached the table. Not waiting for an answer, she poured the hot brew into his cup. "Do you usually eat this slowly?"

"When I told you I didn't have anything better to do, I wasn't kidding." Hearing nothing from the peanut gallery, he thought he might prod a bit. "When do the Lions bowl. You know, the Milltown Lions."

"Don't know. I never paid too much attention. The kids hang out whether they're bowling or not. They like it here. It gives them a place to congregate after school." Her expression changed. "Who are you looking for?"

"No one in particular," he changed his tactic. "I read they are the team to beat, and I thought I'd stick around to watch them play."

Walking toward the kitchen, she pushed open the swinging door with her elbow. "Anyone here know when the Lions team is up?" She dropped the tray of used dishes on the counter. Receiving no answer, she raised her voice and repeated the question. She walked back in Brian's direction. "No one knows," she said as she passed his table. "We do our job here and don't pay too much attention to details."

Brian thought he might leave. He placed down his cup and began to rise from his seat. He stepped out of the booth, in time to see a new group of teens come charging into the cafe. He listened as the students sat to place their orders. Hearing various names being called out, he gave up hope when Sean's name did not come up. As he walked to the exit door, he heard a young teen call out, "Hey, SJ, you're late as usual." Brian eyed the impatient teen as he called out to his friend.

"Sorry, Guys, I got held up with the coach. You know how it is," said the tall, handsome, young man who entered the restaurant.

"You're here now. That's all that counts." The teen appeared relieved. "We've got to get cracking if we're going to beat Bayview."

"I'm starved. Mind if I eat something first?" SJ asked. "You guys see if our lanes are available. I'll only be a few minutes." He found an empty stool at the end of the counter and motioned to the waitress handing Brian his check.

Brian exited the bowling alley and returned to his car. Was he defeated? He sat in the driver's seat for a few minutes thinking of his next move. Then reality hit him. *Suppose SJ stands for Sean James.* He had seen Sean's middle name when searching out columns in the local paper's sports section. Knowing he couldn't leave the alley without investigating further, he jumped out of the car and headed back to the lanes. Once inside, he noticed the same teens he had observed in the cafe huddled around one of the lanes. The boy they called SJ was not there. Impulsively he approached them. "Excuse me. Are any of you on the Lions team?"

"Yeah, we all are," one of them answered. "What's it to you?"

"I should introduce myself. My name is Brian, and I'm interested in picking up a few pointers to improve my score. I was reading about how on fire your team has been, and I was wondering if any one of you would mind—I guess you could call it—tutoring me. Would one of you be willing to give me a few pointers?"

Knowing it could mean spending money, the teens ears perked up. "I'll be happy to pay for it." He gave them a wide smile. "Who's up for it?"

SJ returned from eating his lunch. Hearing the offer and not wanting to give up his spare time to a stranger, he did not respond. His best friend, who had chided him earlier for being late, pointed at Sean. "He's your man." He offered a grin to his buddy. "This is my friend Sean, and he's the best we've got." Introducing himself, he extended his hand to Brian. "I'm Andy."

Brian picked up on Sean's demeanor and tried to soften the situation. Turning to Andy, he said, "How about you doing the teaching, and maybe your friend here would like to come along for the ride? Maybe he can add a pointer or two. What do you say, Guys? How does twenty dollars an hour sound?" Andy's eyes widened. He shot a glance at Sean.

"Sounds pretty good to me, SJ, what do you say, buddy? I need the company."

"Whatever," Sean replied.

"When do we start?" Andy asked.

"What about tomorrow? If your friend comes along and gives me a few tips of his own, I may be willing to double the price."

Sean knew he would have to first discuss it with his dad. He had been saving for a second hand car, and the money sounded good. He knew it would take the pressure off his father if he were able to pay for it himself. He also knew his father would question who this stranger was who seemed to be pressing for an answer. "Can I let you know tomorrow?" he asked Andy.

Andy shot a glance at Brian. "Is that okay with you?"

"Why not, I'll meet you here tomorrow—same time."

"That works for me," Andy's grin was wide.

It would take Sean part of the night to convince himself to show up the next afternoon. *What harm could come from it, helping another guy out?*

~ CHAPTER SIXTEEN ~

It was after midnight when Marge stepped into the elevator at Filtrec
Electronics Corp. She was able to get past the guard without incident
by telling him she had come from the hospital to retrieve some of
Harry's files. She exited onto the sixth floor, stopping for a moment. She
couldn't remember the last time she had visited Harry at work or the
reason for her being there, but she did remember his office was situated
at the end of the hallway, close to the fire exit.

She found her way and was grateful the hallway lights were on. Her
hands began to shake as she fumbled for the largest key, the one that
would open the door to Harry's private world.

Marge felt guilty being there. However, she was determined to find a
clue as to why Harry seemed so distant and stressed out before his heart
attack. As she entered his office, the light from the hallway cast a narrow
beam across the room that disappeared when she closed the door. She
stood in the darkened room for a few seconds. She slid her hand against
the cold plaster wall until her fingers found the light switch.

The room was a perfect square. A reception desk was on one side,
and an el-shaped leather sectional that took most of the space on the
opposite two walls. Both sections were flanked with tables that held
a variety of magazines and two brass lamps with burlap shades. She

retrieved a second key and entered Harry's office. Turning on the light, she fondled her way through her purse until she found the smallest key, the one that would open his massive mahogany desk. She carefully slid the key into the lock of its top drawer and pulled it open. Its contents did not surprise her. The drawer held many of Harry's personal items—a hairbrush and comb, some pipe tobacco, a razor, aftershave, a toothbrush and toothpaste along with a small calendar, several pens, an appointment book and some paper clips. *Nothing earth shaking here.*

She continued her search by opening two of the side drawers that flanked the desk's kneehole space. She found nothing. Finally, she focused on the long drawer to the bottom right of the desk. The drawer was deeper than the others and had a brass keyhole identical to the top drawer. Marge attempted to open it with the same key. It didn't work. "This drawer must be holding files," she whispered. "There must be something of significance here; he must have hidden the key."

She tried to imagine where she would hide something if she had to. Her eyes scanned the room, and she began to investigate every nook and cranny, lifting knick-knacks, statuettes and even searching behind the wall hangings.

About 45 minutes into her quest, Marge noticed a small space between two sets of books. They were housed on mahogany shelves on the opposite wall. Slipping her index finger through the space, she slid out a small silver key. "This has to be it." She returned to the desk.

The key was a perfect fit. Her heart raced as she pulled out the drawer. It held several files attached together with an elastic band. She sat in Harry's black leather chair, and gave herself a few seconds before she pulled out the first file from the stack. She opened it and began to read. "Why these are not client files," she murmured, "These are his personal accounts of bank deposits." She skimmed through them; the picture became clearer. She gasped, removed her glasses, and brushed her hair back from her face.

It was evident Harry was depositing checks into personal accounts, using various banks outside of the United States. Most were in Canada and Europe. He also had several deposits in Dubai. Each entry was documented in his name. There was no mention of Filtrec Electronics Corp. Marge carefully placed the files in the plastic bag she had taken from Harry's hospital room, locked the drawers of the desk, and returned the keys to her purse. As she entered the lobby, she was able to slip past the dozing security guard with his feet elevated on the desk and his head bobbing. Returning to her car, Marge sat there for at least ten minutes. As the reality of his double life set in, her welled up tears flooded her cheeks. "No wonder he was so stressed out," she cried.

Once home, she placed the files in Harry's desk. Finding no solace in her eight-year old calico Daisy, she carried the cat to her room and placed her on the chair next to the window. Too tired to undress, she threw herself across her bed. Unable to find sleep, she cried out to God.

~ CHAPTER SEVENTEEN ~

Both Women beamed as the waiter ushered them into the hotel dining room. "I'm so proud of you, Mom. You kept within your budget." A huge grin erupted across Niki's face. Sensing that her mother was not paying attention, she repeated the compliment.

"Not so," Sarah answered, "I'm about fifty euros over."

They chuckled as they reminisced over their successful shopping spree, which began in the hotel's gift boutique and ended in the late afternoon in downtown London.

The waiter seated the ladies next to a large picture window that offered a view of the main street. Niki eyed the Londoners through the glass as they walked briskly toward the underground station nearby. "Everyone's in such a hurry, just like home. I wish we could all calm down."

Sarah ignored her daughter's comments. "Why this menu is in French. How am I supposed to order breakfast?" She handed the menu to Niki. "You pick something. I'm lost. At least you had French in high school."

Niki took the menu from her mother. The waiter realized his mistake and returned with another set of menus. He retrieved the menus from Niki. "Sorry, Mademoiselle." His face was a bit ruddy. "I'm usually not this forgetful. I'll give you a few moments to decide." With a slight bow, he turned away leaving the two women alone.

After enjoying their meal along with a second cup of coffee, the waiter approached them with a tray of fruit and cheeses. "A peace offering." He smiled. "Please do try our White Stilton with apricots on some crackers—compliments of the hotel."

Niki took a small cluster of succulent grapes and placed them on her plate. An uneasy feeling crept over her. She glanced over Sarah's shoulder into the eyes of the gentleman seated at a far corner of the room. His steady gaze caused her to squirm slightly in her chair. "How did he know we would be here at this hotel?" she whispered. "Why didn't he call me first?"

It took a few seconds for Sarah to catch on. "Do you mean who I think you mean?"

Before her daughter could respond, Chen Young approached the two women and smiled. "Mind if I take a seat?" he asked politely.

"Please do—I wish you had let us know you were coming," Niki responded, her tone also polite.

"It was a bit presumptuous of me," he said, "but I didn't want a rain check."

"I would not have given you one. We could have set a time to meet." Her tone heightened. "We have plans today."

Sensing her annoyance and not wanting to lose the day with Niki, Chen turned to Sarah. "Do you mind if I steal your daughter today since I have only a few days of leisure left in London?"

Trying to hide her disappointment, Sarah remained cordial. She glanced over at Niki, giving her the opportunity to respond for herself.

Niki took a few moments to decide. "Mom, would you mind if I spent the day with Mr. Young. It'll give you a chance to take in the spa."

"You're right. You two youngsters go and have a good time. I'll catch up with her tomorrow." Sarah glanced at Chen.

As they were leaving the dining room, the pair passed through the hotel lobby. Chen caught a glimpse of himself in the ornate mirror that hung over a black granite fireplace. He focused on Niki's reflection and how radiant she looked. Her auburn hair was piled high atop her head in a long-twisted fashion, complimenting the iridescent green two-piece slacks suit that hung magnificently on her size five frame. A large smile illuminated his oval face, which revealed his pure white teeth that had become the brunt of many jokes by his colleagues back home. He was certain they were jealous of his inherited gifts so from time to time in retaliation he would slip whitening toothpaste into each one's locker. He took Niki's hand, and the young couple smiled at each other as they exited the hotel. He waved down a taxi, and with no other thoughts lingering, the couple sped away.

Chen had planned the perfect day. He had done his research of the usual tourist attractions and thought he would begin with a tour of Tower Bridge, Westminster Abbey, and the Clock Tower, commonly known as Big Ben. Then it was off to Harrods and Selfridges to buy some small tokens for the folks back home. Niki agreed with the itinerary. She had always wanted to shop at Selfridges. Being able to visit both department stores was an exhilarating experience for her.

Their day ended with an early dinner at a London pub, a short distance from the hotel. Something had been gnawing at Niki all afternoon, and she wanted to clear it up before they parted in the evening. "How did you know where I was staying?"

"When you returned your wallet to your purse at the market, I saw the hotel key. I hope you are not angry with me for showing up like that."

Satisfied with his excuse and wanting to know more about this stranger, Niki began to delve into his background with the same enthusiasm an author would have researching his novel. There was an attraction she couldn't deny. She began to zero in on those closest to him, as well as his acquaintances. By having some knowledge of who he hung out with, she would know if he was a man of true character.

"Tell me a little about your work," Niki placed her coffee cup down. "What exactly do you do?"

"As I said, I'm in the computer business," Chen lied. "I work for Alcroft Software, a company that develops educational software for college students. Our goal is to help them get through the rough times without paying a tutor. We are still up and coming but doing well in the States. I've been with them for about two years. As the fall semesters are about to begin, I asked my CEO if I could bring our software to the UK. They unanimously agreed to give England a shot. They arranged for me to meet with several college boards here in London. If all goes well, we will bring our product to some of the European countries — in their own languages, of course."

Chen could not take his eyes off Niki the entire evening. As he watched her finish dessert, he continued. "Our software sales hit its peak last week, so I hopped a plane on Monday with my company's blessing, of course, and here I am."

"What do you do in your spare time besides taking a business trip to London?"

"Not much to speak of. My job takes up most of it."

"Were you born in the States?"

Chen was uncomfortable lying to Niki about his work so he decided to answer truthfully anything else she might ask him. "No, I was born in China and moved to the States to attend college. And you?"

"My life is filled with work, church, and goals I haven't achieved yet. I work for a lawyer, I'm a paralegal. We can discuss that another time. I'd like to hear more about how you came here."

Niki searched Chen's eyes as he filled her in on his education and friendships. She tried to glean some certainty to all he was saying, yet she could not shake the feeling that something was amiss. Despite this, she found herself developing some kind of a rapport with this stranger.

Sarah stepped out of the shower in time to hear the news report: "Several armed officers were shot today on the London streets." The Newscaster was shaken, "Unsure if this was an act of terrorism, SAS soldiers have been deployed to bolster security in the city's capital. An ongoing investigation continues, and we will bring you the details as we receive them."

"I wonder if Niki has heard the sad news." Sarah's mood turned somber.

The flight home, though smooth, seemed longer than when they flew to Britain. Niki reflected on the events of the past two weeks, including the news that had disturbed all of London." We have something to pray about, Mom." Sarah agreed. She never mentioned her new friend, which her mother found unusual. Chen captured every thought she had for the remainder of the flight.

The flight attendant interrupted the ladies. "Would you like something to drink?" she asked. "We have coffee, tea, bottled water, soda, and a variety of snacks."

"No, thank you," Niki said. She turned to her mother and gently poked her arm. "Would you like a snack or something to drink?"

"No, thanks," Sarah grunted, "I'd rather sleep."

After a short nap, Sarah sat and refreshed herself with the hot towel offered. She turned to Niki, engrossed in a travel magazine. "What do you think of your new acquaintance?" she asked.

"He's nice, Mom, and he seems dedicated to his work."

"Did this new friendship end in London?"

"As a matter of fact, he's going to call me later this week." Niki stared at her mother for a few seconds, waiting for a reaction. There was none. "Aren't you going to say anything?"

"He seems like a nice guy, Niki. I would need more time to make a judgment on his character."

"You will find out soon enough because he asked if he could take me to dinner next weekend."

The plane touched down several minutes late to a slippery, wet runway. They were the first ones out of their seats. "Grab my overnight and hand it to me please," Sarah requested.

Niki lifted the compartment lid above her and pulled down two overnight cases. She handed one to her mother. She was not looking forward to the long drive home, and she was grateful she would not be the one driving. She sighed, "I hope the limo is on time. We'll have enough to deal with on the parkway in all this rain."

~ CHAPTER EIGHTEEN ~

It was almost one a.m., when Marge received the call. Harry had taken
a turn for the worse and had succumbed to his illness. The doctor
described it as a massive heart seizure. Hearing these fatal words, Marge
grabbed on to the bedpost.

Doctor Roger Saffrin, Chief of Surgery, could be heard on the other end
of the line. "I'm so sorry for your loss, Mrs. Bernside. We tried to reach
you earlier. We need you to come to the hospital as soon as possible."

The receiver dropped from Marge's hand. Unable to speak, she threw
herself on the bed and sobbed, leaving the caller with one choice—to
hang up.

Marge was the first to arrive at Mercy Medical Center. She had
notified her children who planned to meet her there. Not wanting to go
up to Harry's room alone, she decided to wait in the main lobby until
her children arrived. *Maybe things are better this way,* she thought.
Whatever he was involved in, it cannot touch him now. Wiping the
tears from her eyes, she was interrupted by her daughter's voice. "Oh,
Jennifer," she sobbed, "what will we do without him?"

Following close behind his sister was Marge's son Harold, Jr. Seeing
the two women standing in the lobby clinging to one another, he circled
his long arms around them and held them tight. "Mom, I'm so sorry," he

repeated over and over.

The family was visited by Dr. Saul Abraham, the head cardiologist. Dr. Abraham offered his hand to each member of the family and filled them in on some of the details. "We had stabilized him when he was brought in, and we scheduled an angioplasty for tomorrow, but the damage to his heart was too great, and he succumbed to it. We are so sorry we couldn't do more."

Marge had made up her mind she would never divulge Harry's secret life to her children. *What's the sense of it—any respect they had for him would be gone.* Harry, Jr. was following in his father's footsteps and on his way to becoming a top executive in his firm. She decided to remain silent on the matter and prayed Harry's secrets would be buried with him.

The Restful Chapel was located on the edge of town, close to the electrical plants. The taxi driver was new to the area and had some difficulty finding the funeral home. He blamed it on the one-way streets. "It's my first day on the job," he said in his Middle Eastern accent. Tex took it in stride, practicing his entrance speech in the extra time allotted.

As he entered the chapel, he was greeted by the proprietor, a short balding man who solemnly held out his hand. He grinned. "Welcome to Restful. How may I direct you?"

"I'm here to pay my respects, Sir. Can you direct me to the Bernside family?"

"Down the hall to your left." He pointed.

Saying nothing, Tex shook hands with the man and walked slowly along the hallway. He paced himself, as he studied his lines. As best he could, he held on to his forlorn expression and stepped into the viewing room. Several heads turned toward him as he entered. Catching the puzzled looks on some of the faces in the crowd, he began to sweat. Not knowing who Marge was made it more difficult. He took a chance and approached the only elderly woman sitting in the front row across from the casket. She was sobbing softly. He walked over to her and stretched out his hand. His lies flowed as smooth as sea glass. "Mrs. Bernside?"

"Yes, I'm Marge Bernside."

The smell of the floral arrangements turned his stomach. The nausea began to overtake him, and Tex found it difficult to maintain his composure.

"Mrs. Bernside, I'm so sorry for your loss."

"Do I know you—I don't think—"

"Harry talked of you whenever we ran into each other," he interrupted, "and I might add, so lovingly."

"How did you know my Harry?"

"We met when he was on a business trip for Filtrec. I'm an electrical engineer with the southern division of the company. We sat across from each other at a convention we attended many years ago. From time to time when I traveled, I would bump into him. I happen to be in town and read Harry had succumbed to a heart attack. I could not leave Phoenix without paying my respects. I'm Thomas Black, but my friends know me as Tex."

Marge smiled and took his hand. "Why, Mr. Black, it's so kind of you to go out of your way to come here tonight. Please know I appreciate your coming."

"I'll be staying at the Westerner Inn in town if you ever need anything—anything at all. I'd be happy to oblige." Tex patted her hand. "I must be going—business you know. Please feel free to call me if I can be of any service to you." Taking his calling card from his inside jacket pocket, he handed it to Marge. Tex knew how to charm women; he was a natural at it, and his tall frame and good looks didn't hinder the process. She nodded and thanked him.

His taxi was right on time. The experienced driver brought him back to his hotel in half the time it took to reach the chapel. Satisfied his encounter with Marge went well, the only choice he had was to wait and see if she would contact him. He booked his stay for one week in hopes she would respond to his offer of assistance. He decided if he didn't hear from her within that time, he would resort to Plan B.

Marge was not used to doing things on her own. Harry attended to most of the household responsibilities, which left little for her to contend with. It had been more than a week since the funeral, and she was still unable to focus. Harry, Jr. created a large calendar for her and pinned it on the kitchen wallboard. He charted when each bill was due along with things that related to her daily living—doctors' appointments, hair salon appointments, and her meetings with the garden club. He even charted when the oil change on her car was due, although he usually did it himself. Birthdays of relatives were marked in red ink, several days before the actual date, to give her time to send a card. Marge had a thing about sending cards to each relative, even distant cousins' on time. Yet, she hadn't looked at the calendar once and was sinking deeper and deeper into a depression.

Harry had been known for being impeccably dressed so Marge decided to donate some of his clothing to her church's thrift shop. One morning, after going through some of their personal belongings, she came across the black dress she had worn to the viewing. Not wanting to wear it again, she carefully folded it and placed it in a plastic bag along with some of Harry's clothing. She hoped it would not be worn for the same reason. Upon folding it, a card fell out of its front pocket and dropped unnoticed onto the bedroom floor. She placed the clothing into the trunk of her car to deliver it to the thrift shop the following morning. Exhausted, she returned to her bedroom and sat on an easy chair near the window. She reached for her reading glasses and the Daily Sun Journal on her nightstand. Noticing a small card lying face down on the scatter rug, she picked it up. At first glance, she did not recognize the name on the card and attempted to tear it up. Suddenly, it dawned on her. *It may belong to that handsome stranger that came to the viewing.* She clutched the tiny card for a moment, and placed it in her purse. She read until she drifted off into a needed slumber.

Tex delayed his flight for several days before returning to Houston. He had promised Joe he would finish his assignment, but his Puerto Rican experience, which he had considered a waste of time, left a bad taste in his mouth. He even thought of calling Neva to see if she survived her fall in the garden. *I was starting to take a liking to the ol' gal,* he thought. Now, Joe has given him another older woman to scrutinize. Putting his own business aside to help an old friend is one thing — tracking down 50 to 80 something's, who happen to be grandmothers, was another. It was beginning to cross a line with him.

Marge was having a difficult time adjusting to being alone. She didn't want to become dependent on her children so she tried to occupy her days as much as possible. She joined the local ladies' league in town.

It kept her busy a few afternoons a month, and there was always her sewing and garden clubs and the Teal Hat Society. Yet, the time she spent in solitude still devastated her.

A month had gone by since Harry's passing. It was a downcast Saturday afternoon. Marge decided she would avoid the predicted downpour and settle in with a good book. She poured herself a cup of herbal tea and climbed the stairs to her bedroom with her book in hand. She kicked off her slippers and stretched out on the gold velvet settee near the side of her bed. She absorbed herself in her novel for several hours. The sound of chimes from the grandfather clock, bellowing in the hallway below, reminded her of the time. "Oh Lord, I almost forgot. I promised the kids I would babysit tonight." Grateful she would have less time to think about facing another night alone, she showered and dressed. In less than an hour, she found herself at Harry, Jr.'s front door.

~ CHAPTER NINETEEN ~

Unnoticed, Neva lay on the ground for at least two hours before she came to. Her exposed skin was reddened by the tropical sun. She rolled over on her back and lifted her right arm over her eyes to protect them from its glare. At the same moment, Alma, her friend and neighbor of thirty years, had woken from an afternoon nap. She opened her blind and peered out to greet the afternoon. As her eyes adjusted to the light, she noticed the large figure lying helplessly in the yard. "Oh, my Lord," she cried. She bolted out the back door and ran to her friend's side.

Neva and Alma had sustained a close relationship for the many years they had lived in San Juan, and the two had become inseparable— shopping, eating, and traveling together. A day did not go by where one of them would not check on the other. Alma was sorry she overslept. Reaching Neva's side, she attempted to lift her friend. Her efforts failed. "Neva, are you alright?" she cried. "What happened?"

Disoriented, Neva tried to support herself by leaning on Alma's shoulder. Slipping several times, they managed to walk toward the back door and into the house. Alma steered her into the kitchen and seated her down on one of the old wooden chairs. Neva's hands cradled her head, swaying it back and forth like a pendulum, as if she was testing it to see if it was still attached. Alma touched Neva's head to check for any injuries. She gasped as her fingers palpated a large lump directly above her left temple. "Oh, Lord, you are hurt. You've been injured." She quickly pulled the ice tray from the refrigerator and placed several cubes into a plastic bag. She covered the lump and placed Neva's hand over the bag to hold it in place.

"Can you remember anything," Alma asked. "How did you fall? What happened?"

Neva, still unable to recall what led to that moment, responded, "I must have gotten dizzy. The sun—it was so hot."

After nursing Neva for at least half an hour, Alma walked her into her bedroom and placed her on the bed. "I'm going to call Dr. Ottorro, Neva. He'll come—he'll help you, okay?" Neva muttered something and began to drift off. Alma picked up the phone and dialed the old physician who had been the town's caregiver for as long as both women had lived on the island. After the call, Alma walked over to the bed and bent over and kissed Neva gently on the forehead. "Doctor will be here within the hour," she whispered. "You rest. I'll be right by the window." She took a seat on the window bench and gazed out at the lovely garden, the apple of her dearest friend's eye.

Alma was short in stature. Her friendly eyes were dark and small. She maintained the same twinkle in them as Neva's eyes had. Unlike her friend's white coiffed hair, her grey hair, streaked with black, was worn in braids that were pinned up to encircle her narrow face. The two had developed a friendship when Alma first arrived on the island.

Alma's husband was a Christian missionary who ran a small mission for impoverished children until his passing. Neva had joined their church and helped to teach Bible stories to the children when time would allow. Their bond became stronger as they continued to look out for each other's well-being.

Alma awaited the doctor's arrival. She gazed out at the garden Neva had tended to for so long and reminisced of better times—busy days and nights of ministering to her children, as she called them, although, like her good friend, she had no children of her own.

~ CHAPTER TWENTY ~

Niki reached the porch steps before the predicted downpour. She was grateful she had made it home in time. She loved the sound of rain on the roof and the smell of the wet grass when the showers ended. She preferred to be inside looking out on days like this. On occasion with a lighter shower, she would take short walks, and when there was no threat of lightning, she would stroll through the park with her umbrella to take in the vibrancy the rain brought. She appreciated the fact the landscape always looked more colorful when it rained. This was no ordinary shower. She dashed into the kitchen, dropped her packages on the counter, and ran to the open windows to shut them tightly.

Five minutes hadn't passed when the doorbell rang. Thunder crashed. The torrent hit the roof of the house with a vengeance." Who on earth would dare to go out in this?" she murmured. She was surprised when a gentleman in uniform stood before her with a bouquet of flowers.

Who would be sending flowers on a non-occasion? Curious, she thanked the man, signed the receipt, and walked to the kitchen. She removed her favorite ceramic vase from the cabinet and filled it halfway with water. Cutting each stem on an angle, she arranged the flowers, placing the tallest ones in the middle of the vase and surrounding them with the smaller ones. She decided she would wait for her mother to arrive before opening the small envelope. *After all, the flowers could be for Mom.*

Sarah was caught in traffic during the cloudburst. The local roads began to flood. She arrived home a few minutes after 7 p.m.; her suit and shoes were drenched. Niki gave her mother enough time to remove her wet clothing and settle in. "Mom, a bouquet of flowers arrived today," she said. "I signed for them, but I didn't open the card—I wanted to wait for you to get home. I can't imagine who would be sending flowers."

Sarah stepped into the dining room and inspected the gorgeous arrangement of carnations, roses, and sweet baby's breath, which Niki had placed on the table. "Open the card, Niki, let's see who they are from."

Niki withdrew a small white envelope from the bouquet and opened it. She read aloud. "To a sweet girl. I'm looking forward to seeing you again. Thanks for London." The message was typed, and it was signed personally by Chen Young.

"Are you going to tell me who they are from?" Sarah asked as if she didn't know.

"Maybe later," Niki teased. "Come on, Mom. Dinner's on. Let's eat."

Although Niki had been raised in a Christian environment, it was not the same for Sarah, who had come to know Christ at a later time in her life. After a long illness, a friend suggested she attend a prayer meeting in the home of a neighbor. Although unwilling at first, Sarah was desperate to find healing of both body and soul. She agreed to go. What she experienced inside that home was a miracle. Her heart was ready to surrender to God. She thought she knew Him, yet she had never experienced Him in such a personal way. The rest was history. She continued her journey with Him, knowing for her, there was no other way—no turning back.

Niki had found Christ at an early age. She attended church and bible studies faithfully. She knew how important it was to herself and to her mother to remain strong in her faith, and she was not ready to entertain any thought of falling for a non-believer. She knew nothing of Chen Young's religious convictions. It was too soon to delve deeper into his personal life. Right, or wrong, she would give it more time.

Chen had been looking forward to his next date with Niki and hoped she would call and thank him for the flowers. He was delighted when the call came.

Niki lowered her voice and tried to hide her excitement. "Hello Chen, this is Niki. I received your flowers and wanted to thank you personally."

"I was hoping you would call." Chen couldn't help but smile, even though the thought she may refuse to see him haunted him. He knew she would never continue to date him if she knew he was involved in drug trafficking. He was not a drug user, and he had never done anything like this before. His connection with Joe Balboa had put money in his pocket, an offer he couldn't refuse. He tried to convince himself not to let his emotions get the better of him, but after his first encounter with Niki in the London flea market, things had changed. It only took one date of exploring London with her to realize he was beginning to fall for her. Their conversation ended after it was agreed Chen would pick her up the following Friday.

Niki could hardly wait for Friday evening to arrive. The doorbell rang at precisely eight-thirty. Stopping only to compose herself, Niki raced to the door. Chen looked handsome, she thought, in his dark grey suit, white shirt and green and blue-print tie. He had mentioned dinner out and a movie; however, he was not dressed for a routine trip to the local theatre.

"I didn't know you were going to dress up. Would you mind if I ran upstairs and changed?" she asked.

"Yes, I would mind. You look fine." He grabbed her hand and smiled as he pulled her toward the front door.

Niki had dressed in a basic black dress with a patent leather belt and low black pumps. The only jewelry she wore that evening was a sapphire cross she rarely removed from her neck. In case Chen decided to take her somewhere after the movie, she knew a black dress would be passable. She arranged her long hair on top of her head in a bun with ringlets cascading on both sides of her face, which gave her a dressier look.

The young couple arrived at the Greenbay Country Club around 9 p.m. Niki was impressed with the place but confused. "I thought we were going to dinner and a movie?" she asked.

"I wanted this night to be special, Niki. There's something I want to discuss with you." In a way his words frightened her. They sounded warm and personal, but until she knew of his religious convictions, she had decided she would not encourage a long-term relationship. Being friends would suffice.

"Do you belong to this club?" Niki asked.

"As a matter of fact, I don't. An old friend of mine moved into this area and joined it last year. We are his guests for the evening. He comes here at least twice a week to play golf, and whenever I'm in town, we have a game — weather permitting."

"Please thank him for me."

Niki admired the paintings that adorned the walls in the massive lobby. The largest one was centered above the seating area. Walnut paneling complimented the ornate crystal chandeliers that dotted the ceiling, sparkling in the soft light. Leather chairs flanked a round mahogany table, where a huge hand cut crystal vase stood holding an arrangement of fresh cut chrysanthemums of various shades.

"Is it a special occasion?" Her expression puzzled. "I had no idea we were coming to such a place. I hope I'm dressed ok."

"Shush, be quiet." Chen clutched her hand. "When we get seated, we can talk," he whispered. He was about to tell her something he dreaded. He hoped taking her to a special place would soften the blow. He was about to find out.

Chen requested the waiter seat them away from the noise of the kitchen. Taking longer than usual to choose an entree, Niki apologized to the waiter. "Not a problem, Miss. I'll give you a few more moments to decide." He turned toward the kitchen and left the couple alone. Niki was uncomfortable as she glanced at the prices on the menu." Will you order for me tonight? I like almost anything."

"I don't mind, but please be honest if you don't like what I choose." Chen smiled and motioned for the waiter to return to their table. He could not take his eyes off of Niki that evening. Half-way through the dinner he made his move. "Niki, I wanted tonight to be a special time for us. I have something I have to tell you, and I don't know how you will receive it. I want you to know that no matter the outcome, it will not change my feelings for you."

A pink tinge erupted on her cheeks and her hands became moist.

Her heart raced as she listened, clueless to what he was about to divulge.

"I've grown fond of you, Niki" He took her hand in his. "I think you know, by now. I haven't been honest with you. I'm not a software executive, I'm a detective. I work for the Camwood Police Department."

Niki sighed with relief. "Is that all. I thought you were going to confess a crime." Then it hit her." Wait a minute. I was in Camwood this past August. This is not a coincidence—you and I meeting?" Her expression changed from one of worry to one of deep hurt. "Did you follow me to London? I already told Sergeant O'Donnell everything I knew. What exactly do you want from me?"

Chen's adrenaline kicked in and began to flood his system. He could feel his heart pound within his chest. "Let me finish, please." He was holding on to her hand. "I've been with the sarge more than a year. The first year went well for me, but I got in the wrong company at work, and hung out with some not so nice officers. They are greedy men who will stop at nothing to get what they want. They..."

"And what is it they want?" Niki interrupted.

"Drugs and money." The answer came fast and unexpected.

"How does this involve you?" Niki tried to mask her emotions.

"They drew me in, and I began to lead a double life," he explained. "I started out arresting the drug pushers in Chinatown, and later, I was offered mega bucks for turning my head. I liked the perks. I had the best of each world, a good job where I was respected, and a way to make easy money. It wasn't long after, I started running for them. I wasn't buying or selling, I was delivering the goods. I became their courier."

Niki sat there unable to speak. Her mind went in all directions. She remained mute. Her new world began to crumble.

Suddenly, it dawned on Chen what Niki had revealed to him. His heart dropped to his stomach. *It's her. She's the one Joe is looking for. She's the one who witnessed the transaction in the parking lot.* It took a few minutes for both to gain composure.

"Please go on," she said.

Chen managed to continue, "I loved my life. I was living on the edge and I knew it, that is, until I met you. I can see you are a woman of faith. Watching you live your life, and seeing how committed you are, has turned my life around." He didn't wait for a response. "I want the peace you seem to have deep inside you. I know I have no right to ask or even hope, but if you will continue to see me, I promise I will sever all ties I have with the underworld."

"You know I've had you in my prayers since we met. I want to reassure you of that." She pulled her hand from his." I had planned tonight to share some thoughts I've had about our relationship. I will put that on hold for awhile."

"Please tell me. What feelings?" he asked.

Niki tried to smile—she was unable. "I am disappointed in what you have told me. I can't give you hope right now for us to continue our relationship." She touched his hand. "I am willing to share my faith with you if you will allow me."

Chen was silent. Niki gave him a few minutes to take it all in. His expression remained unchanged. "You need Christ in your life more than anything right now. You need His guidance and direction not only from a good pastor but from God's Word itself. It's easy to say, "I repent." For me to continue a relationship with you, I would have to see the fruit of this repentance, and that will take time—a lot of time." Her voice became stronger. "You would have to sever all your ties to these people, including the fellow officers who are involved. You would have to repent of all those you have hurt along the way, because by turning your head many young people have been affected. You made it easier for them to get the drugs, and if they weren't hooked yet, you put more drugs out on the street as bait for the once innocent who are dragged into this lifestyle by the devil himself."

Her words left Chen speechless. He bowed his head as if he were praying. "Please allow me some space," Niki requested. "And, when you are ready to commit your life to Christ, call me. I will arrange for you to meet with my pastor." Unable to finish her dinner, she asked to be taken home.

Chen did not notice the tears streaming down Niki's cheeks as she stepped into his car that evening. She kept her face toward the window during the drive home. They pulled up to her house in the dark of night, and she gracefully said goodnight. She did not wait for Chen to open the door for her. She stepped out of the car and dashed to her front door alone. She never looked back.

~ CHAPTER TWENTY–ONE ~

Joe hung up the den phone. His conversation with Chen did not go as planned. He had no idea he was seeing Niki on a personal level, and the last thing Chen wanted was for Joe to find out. His feelings for Niki were becoming stronger with each date. He was unable to deny them even to himself. He knew he would never betray her.

"How are you doing with the Hughes girl," Joe asked.

"Dead end, Joe. You've got the wrong girl."

Joe was annoyed, yet another time he didn't score. "Listen Chen, there's a couple on my list that was in Camwood that night. The old man died recently, and I have Tex on it. He's gutless when it comes to old folk, so I need you as a backup in case he caves." There was silence. "Hey, did you hear a word I've said?"

"I heard you, Joe. You want me to kill someone. Right? I told you, I'd do the running for you. Murder is not in my vocabulary. I don't want to get involved in this any longer."

"You're in this as deep as the rest of us. You can't back out now. If you do, I'll dump the whole thing in your lap. You know the department is under investigation as we speak. And it'll all be yours if you fail to cooperate. Brian and I will deny everything, and you'll be holding the bag. Someone saw us that night in Camwood, and they can identify us. You included, Einstein." Joe continued, "If the Hughes girl and her mother are off the list and Brian clears the camera freak and his son, there's a good chance it's the Bernside woman or her dead husband. And I can't grill him now, can I? If Tex bails, I need a back up."

"I'll call you later." Chen hung up before Joe could respond.

As Joe heard the click in his ear, something told him it was more than the conversation he had with Chen Young that was over.

~ CHAPTER TWENTY–TWO ~

It had been almost two weeks since Brian began frequenting the Milltown Bowling Alley. His knowledge of the sport began to grow along with his relationship with Sean and Andy. He was making progress, and a night out for some burgers at a local eatery was not unusual for the trio. One evening after a successful game and a trip to Burger Haven, Brian made his move. "Listen, Guys, it's about time I touch base with your families. Don't you think?"

Andy agreed. "Sure, I'll check with my folks, and let you know when."

Sean offered no response, knowing his dad would not be open to older strangers hanging around the team. He decided he would invent an excuse to get himself off the hook. Catching on to Sean's demeanor, Brian turned to the teen. "What about you?"

"My dad works a lot. I'll have to ask when it's a good time."

Brian dropped the subject until one evening during a heavy downpour, he insisted on driving Sean home. As the car entered the driveway, there was Jack, standing in a pool of water, trying to set up a drainage pump.

"Our driveway always floods." Sean looked tense.

Jack could barely see through the torrent. "Is that you, Sean?" he yelled out, not recognizing the car.

"It's me, Dad. I had to beg a ride. I didn't want to drown in this tidal wave."

Jack started the pump and stepped up to the driver's side of the car and tapped on the window. Brian lowered the pane.

"Hello, Mr. Heaton, I'm Brian White. Your son needed a lift, and I volunteered." Unable to overpower the sound of suction coming from the driveway, he repeated the introduction.

"I'm Sean's dad," Jack responded. "Son, aren't you going to ask Mr. White in? Maybe he could use a hot drink? I'd like to thank him personally."

Brian smiled. *Just what the doctor ordered.* "Why, that's kind of you." Shutting the car motor, he stepped out of the sedan and followed Jack and Sean into the house. Once inside, he extended his hand to Jack. "I'm Brian," he repeated, "I'm happy to know you, Mr. Heaton."

"I didn't expect Sean had older friends," Jack said. "I thought you were one of the boys."

"I understand your concern," Brian responded. "Sean and his friend Andy have been tutoring me in the game. I met them at the alley about two weeks ago, and we've become good friends. They have helped me improve my score, and I'm grateful. I was on my way home, and the weather, being so nasty—I hope you don't mind."

"Seeing you have taken such good care of my son, how could I?" Jack said somewhat relieved. "Would you like a hot cup of coffee before you take off?"

"I would appreciate it. Thank you."

Brian was ushered into the living room and told to make himself comfortable. Jack excused himself and started toward the kitchen. Sean, who had gone upstairs to change his wet clothing, returned in a matter of minutes and sat on the fireside chair opposite Brian. It took a few minutes before Jack returned. He was carrying a tray with a carafe of hot coffee, a pitcher of milk, some sugar packets, a dish of chocolate chip cookies, and three mugs. "Help yourself, Mr. White," Jack placed the tray on the coffee table.

Brian was trained to manipulate circumstances, and so he had no trouble deceiving the Heatons. "I know you must have reservations about my befriending the boys, Mr. Heaton."

Jack glanced at Brian sideways.

Brian caught the look. "Your son has been a great help to me. My score has improved at least ten points since he and Andy have been mentoring me." He took the mug of coffee Jack offered, grateful it would buy him some time.

"That's nice to hear," Jack responded.

"Look, why don't we meet for dinner one night soon—my treat. This way you can see my intentions are honorable. I won't be needing the boys much longer. How about it?"

"Why don't you stop over one morning and have breakfast with us?"

"Dad makes awesome pancakes," Sean chimed in, sensing his father's uneasiness. "He says the secret is lots of melted butter and a dash of vanilla."

"Sounds great, but I insist on treating you both to a good steak."

Jack was hesitant. "I'll have Sean give you a call. I'll have to check my appointment book at the studio.

"Wonderful. Please call me Brian."

"You can do the same for me. Jack."

Jack and Sean arrived at Connelly's Pub. It was nearing 7:30 p.m. They were escorted to one of the booths which lined the walls of the main dining room. As they passed the bar, they spotted Brian, seated at the far end on a large wooden stool. Brian was laughing and conversing with the bartender. Not wanting Sean to stand in the bar area, Jack asked the waiter to seat them in the dining room. As his server walked away to retrieve the menus, Jack called out to him to return to their table. "I would appreciate it if you would tell that gentleman seated over there his guests have arrived for dinner," Jack's eyes pointed toward Brian.

"Of course, Sir. I'll take care of it right now."

Jack watched as the waiter approached Brian, and he smiled as Brian looked his way and began strolling to their table.

"Hello, I hope you weren't waiting too long for us," Jack extended his hand.

"Not at all, it gave me a chance to start the night off with a Jack Daniel," Brian quipped. "And how is my best instructor tonight." He turned toward Sean. "Drier than when I last saw you, I hope?" He winked.

"It's raining tonight, but nothing like the other night," Sean replied. "We won't have to get the pump out to clear the driveway. That's for sure."

Brian laughed and took the seat across from Jack. "I appreciate the company tonight, and I insist on picking up the tab. No contest, Gentlemen, please."

Lucy Bella Donna

Jack still had reservations about this new acquaintance of Sean's. He called it a gut feeling and took Brian up on his offer to have dinner with him. He wanted to dig a little deeper into who this stranger was who had befriended his son. He did not open up to Sean about Brian—he knew his son would rebel if he thought he disliked his new friend. It was too late; Sean was already taken in, and Jack knew it.

The conversations began with small talk. After dinner and a few drinks, Brian got right to the point. "Done any traveling lately, Jack?"

"As a matter of fact, yes. Sean and I recently got back from a vacation in the east. Camwood. Have you ever been there?"

"Why no, I hear it's a perfect place to enjoy nature at its best. Sean tells me you're a great photographer. You must have gotten some pretty good shots of the area. I'd love to see them." Finding it hard to pretend, he went on,"I had considered taking a short trip myself after reading a few articles. Believe it or not, Camwood did cross my mind."

"What is it about Camwood that would draw you to the place?" Jack asked.

"Like I said, I hear it is nature at its best. I dabbled in a little photography myself years ago, and I was thinking of taking it up again as a hobby."

"Along with bowling?"

Brian avoided the question. "What better place than Camwood with its lakes and canals and its quaint streets and Ivy League culture. Good photography tells its story. Maybe you can give me some pointers."

"You've done your homework, haven't you." Satisfied Brian had some knowledge of the little town, Jack ended his interrogation.

"And how did you find Camwood, Young Man?" Brian asked the teen. Anything interesting or exciting happen to write about?"

"I had fun with Dad exploring. We did a lot of fishing and canoeing. Dad got some great shots. We stayed at a B&B near the canal."

"Yes, I enlarged several shots with my new lenses. I was able to capture both sunrise and sunsets on the water. They've been displayed in my store window since we got back." Jack was proud.

The rest of the conversation went as planned for Brian, but the outcome was frustrating. It took another half an hour for him to conclude his mission in Milltown was over. In a way, he was relieved. Unsuccessful, in the words uttered by Tex when he left Puerto Rico, Brian's mind echoed, *I'm out of here!*

~ CHAPTER TWENTY-THREE ~

Marge hurried upstairs to check on her grandchildren. "Sorry I'm late, I got caught up in my novel," she yelled back at Harry, Jr., who was standing in the hallway.

"It's ok, Mother. Lisa and I are running a bit late ourselves. The children's dinner is in the oven. See to it they get to bed by eight."

Marge enjoyed watching her grandchildren. They had taken the edge off her anxiety, and she was grateful for time spent with them. After tucking in Alyssa, who had turned seven a month before, she entered nine year old Hannah's room and found her fast asleep. Four year old Leah had climbed into her sister's bed and was also sleeping peacefully. Satisfied all was well, she tiptoed out and down the stairs.

Marge returned to the living room. Noticing a family album on the bottom shelf of the coffee table, she began to skim through the pages. She stopped to look at a picture of her and Harry, Sr., taken on the cruise ship Statendam ten years earlier. *What happier times.* Marge picked up the photo and placed it in the side pocket of her purse. Recognizing Tex's calling card, she pulled it out and studied it for a few seconds. *Maybe he can help me find out about the secret bank accounts Harry had before the authorities do.* From what Tex had told her, he was not involved in the central offices of Filtrec Electronics Corp., working from out of state, but he did have ties with it. After all, no one would suspect if he did some research into the western division of the company. He might even be privy to some of the books.

Tex's phone was vibrating. He stepped out of the shower, grabbed a towel, and rushed to the kitchen area. He swiped his cell phone off the counter in time to answer the caller. "This is Tex. Who's calling?"

"Mr. Black, is that you? This is Marge Bernside. Do you remember me? You were kind enough to come to the viewing when my Harry passed on."

"Why yes, I remember you, Mrs. Bernside. How are you getting along these days? It must be a tough time for you."

"I'm getting along as best I can," Marge replied. "The reason I'm calling is that you offered to be of assistance if I ever needed it, and I am in great need of help."

"I'm in Houston, Mrs. Bernside. Maybe I can help you over the phone. What seems to be the problem?" Tex knew her reply would determine if it was worth a trip back to Phoenix. He listened intently as Marge spoke.

"I'm so sorry, Mr. Black. What I have to say can't be said over the phone. I shouldn't have bothered you."

"No, don't hang up," fearful he would lose the one chance he had to touch base with her—he kept her talking. "Fill me in as best you can. If I need to fly back to Phoenix, I will. Please go on."

Silence followed before the reply came. "You see, Mr. Black, my husband Harry was involved in some embezzlement before he passed on, and I am holding the journals he left behind. I need someone I can trust to go over them with me and help me decide whether I should go to the authorities or not." Marge went on, "I don't want to be liable for anything he may have been involved with, yet, I want to protect the good name he had made for himself. I trust this information is confidential, and will say no more over the phone."

Marge was desperate. She ended the conversation with a lie. "Mr. Black, if you decide to help me, I will make it worth your while. Harry left me in a comfortable position, you know."

"Of course, I will try and help you, Marge—can I call you Marge?" Not waiting for an answer, he rambled on, "I'll have to arrange to fly back, and I will need a few days. I'll be in touch with you. In the meantime, do not talk to anyone about this, not even your children." Before hanging up, he added, "Please, call me Tex."

Tex smiled. He knew this would be an open door for him to get into Marge's head. He could establish a trusting relationship, one that would allow him to ask the personal questions. He hit speed dial on his phone; the voice on the other end bellowed "Balboa here."

"Joe, it's Tex. I just got off the phone with the Bernside woman. I think I have enough on her already to hold her hostage." His laugh was sinister. "I'm flying to Phoenix this weekend. I'll be in touch."

"What do you mean you got something on her? You catch her stealing a car?"

"I'll explain later. I've got to go and make arrangements."

"Before you hang up, you should know something. Chen has hit a dead end. It seems everyone on the list has checked out negative, that is, except the Bernsides. Her husband can't talk now, but she can. If you find out she can identify who was in the parking lot that night, you'll get a bigger cut, and if you get the job done, you'll get half. Sounds good, right?"

Tex was determined to focus on the prize and tried to avoid the fact that annihilating another human being was part of the deal. *I might have hit the jackpot.* Returning to the bedroom, he sat at his computer and logged onto his usual ticket agent. *If I get a coach ticket for the weekend, I should be able to meet with her on Saturday or Sunday.* "Good work, if I say so myself."

~ CHAPTER TWENTY-FOUR ~

Chen arrived home a little after eleven o'clock. He went upstairs
and fell to his knees at the foot of his bed. He cried out to the Lord
for forgiveness and mercy. He knew he could not make up for the
damage he had caused, and he was willing to try to live up to his new
commitment—to turn his life over to Christ. Composing himself, he
picked up the receiver and dialed Joe's number.

The usual "Balboa here," was heard at the opposite end.

"Joe, this is Chen." His voice was stronger than he thought possible.
"I'm calling to tell you that I want out. I don't care what you do about it,
you can threaten me all you want. I want out tonight—right now in fact."

"Do you always do your friends dirty like this? We made a deal."

"Yeah, and murder was not a part of it. Besides, you lied to me. You
led me to believe there was three of us involved—me, you, and Brian.
And now you say there's another. It's your cowboy friend, isn't it? I'm
getting out now before it gets too deep. I only wanted to make a little
cash, and I see now there are other ways—right ways, and I'm going that
route from now on. I gave you what you wanted to know. The Hughes
women know nothing about that night."

"Sounds like you got religion, Chen. You pray, but you better pray
hard because when I get through with you, you'll need those prayers."

Chen hung up the phone and once again fell to his knees. He sobbed. He remembered he hadn't cried like this since he first left his family as a young teenager in China. He was sent to live with his father's brother, and his wife, in the States. His parents hoped he would find a better life. Being a wealthy importer, his uncle offered to cover all his expenses. Chen had remained forever grateful and indebted to them. He never took advantage of the fact things were easy for him. He worked diligently to maintain an A average in order to make his family proud. Now, he was repenting to God for using the talents he had been given dishonestly.

Chen decided his next step would be to wait—to wait on God. He prayed Niki would contact him. He knew he would have to go to his superior and tell him what he was involved in and hope for some leniency. He expected to face jail time. He prayed openly to God, crying out, "Lord, I don't want to continue in the lifestyle I've chosen for myself. I'm ashamed and sorry. Thank you for using Niki in my life. She has allowed me to see what honesty and truth is all about. She has a childlike faith I envy, and I am asking You to put this same childlike faith into my heart. Let me know I am forgiven and help me to forgive myself. I am truly sorry for what I have done. Give me another chance to prove to You, Lord, I am serious in my commitment. I will pay the price for my actions because it can't compare to the price you paid for me." He remembered Niki's words, "With true repentance comes tears."

Chen knew there are consequences to sin that must be paid for in this world, and he was willing to pay them. He didn't grasp the fact, when you ask forgiveness through Christ, sin is not only forgiven, it's forgotten by God. He had to forgive himself. He began to read the Scriptures daily, and as the scales were being removed from his eyes, he grew in his faith. He saw that God had a plan for his life. He was confident God was in complete control, and he left Joe's fate to the Lord, hoping he too would be spiritually convicted of the lifestyle he chose. Chen had been set free. He awaited the world's punishment.

Sarah glanced at the clock on her nightstand when she heard the front door close. Surprised to see it was still early, she slipped out of bed and went downstairs to greet her daughter. "I thought you'd be much later than this. How was your date?"

Still dazed at what Chen had revealed to her, Niki averted the question. "Mom, I'm tired. Can we talk about this in the morning? I want to get to bed."

"I didn't mean to pry. I expected you to arrive home later. The dentist's secretary called to confirm your appointment tomorrow. Have you forgotten? If you want to—"

"No, Mom, I haven't forgotten, and no, I don't want to cancel," Niki interrupted. "I'm going to get some sleep. I'll talk to you in the morning."

Noticing the strained look on Niki's face, Sarah dared not take things any further. "You get a good night's sleep. We'll talk tomorrow."

Relieved, Niki retreated to her room and threw herself on the bed. She had promised herself she would never let a relationship cloud her good sense. She could not help herself, and the tears began to flow freely. She was not aware of her deep feeling for Chen until this night. "Why would he deceive me? What was the motive in that?" she kept repeating. She did not find sleep. She lay on her back for a long time and stared at the ceiling fan, watching it revolve as if she were waiting for it to lull her to sleep. It was after four a.m., when she finally found rest.

The knock on Niki's bedroom door startled her out of her slumber.

"You missed your appointment. I thought you'd be gone by now," Sarah said.

"Sorry, Mom. I overslept. I'll reschedule." Turning over on her side, Niki lay there motionless, hoping her mother would leave. She tried to comprehend the events of the previous evening, and after her usual morning conversation with the Lord, she decided she would no longer contact Chen Young. She would continue to pray for him, and had hoped he listened when she presented him with the way out of his present life, and into a new life in Christ.

~ CHAPTER TWENTY–FIVE ~

Tex's plane arrived at Sky Harbor International Airport on schedule. He grabbed his carry-on bag and rushed to the claim area to pick up his suitcase. As he stood before the carousel, he noticed a figure of short stature waving behind the huge glass window that separated him from the non-travelers. He took a second look and recognized Marge Bernside. His lips curled to one side. He waved then retrieved his belongings.

Tex passed through the exit doors into the waiting area. Marge rushed up to him, still waving. She seemed elated and shook his hand. "Tex, it's so good to see you again. Thank you so much for making the trip."

"Hello, Marge, I'm surprised to see you here. I was going straight to my hotel. I was about to call a cab. How did you find me? I didn't give you any details about my arrival. I was going to call you from my room."

"I had to do a little detective work myself. I thought you might be leaving in the morning, and you did mention the airline you usually book your trip on when we last spoke. I put two and two together, and here I am. Now, please don't give me a hard time. I have plenty of room, and it will give us more time to get acquainted. We can go through the journals I found in the privacy of my home."

"What will your children say? You agreed you didn't want them to know what your husband was involved in." He tried hard to sound concerned. "And, I am a stranger."

"Yes, but you told me you were a business acquaintance of sorts, and that's all they need to know. Besides, my son is away with his family, and my daughter is on a business trip, so I need not say anything for now. You may be gone, by the time they return. Doesn't the Bible say something about being kind to strangers—showing hospitality because some have entertained angels unawares?"

Feeling a twinge of guilt upon Marge referring to Scripture, Tex was quick to change the subject. "You must allow me to take you to dinner while I'm staying with you," he offered, posing his southern charm.

"I parked at Terminal 4." She pointed to the area. "Follow me." Some grey clouds began hovering overhead. "Looks like rain, doesn't it?"

Tex looked up at the dense sky and agreed. "It sure does, Ma'am. I guess we'd better hurry."

It took less than a half an hour to arrive at Marge's residence. Considering the forecast, she had left the lights on. The day had already turned dark and dreary. As they entered the foyer of her home, the sound of rain echoed across the rooftop. It had always had a calming effect on Marge. "Do you like the rain, Tex?" she asked. "I do love the rain."

"Ma'am, there are times I do, and there are times I don't," he said in his thick drawl. "This is a time I don't. Traveling always knocks the wind out of me, and downpours kind of mess up my plans. But we made it in the nick of time, didn't we?" He exposed his amber stained teeth.

"Yes, we did. I know you must be tired, so why don't I show you to your room, and you can settle in. Help yourself to anything you need. There are fresh towels, soap and washcloths in the linen closet next to your bedroom. You can take a hot shower and change. After dinner we can talk. Take your time. The roast won't be ready until seven."

Tex entered the dining room at seven sharp. Marge was pleased and greeted him with a warm smile. "You look well rested as if you haven't been traveling at all. Sit here," she pointed to the chair at the head of the table, "so we can get better acquainted."

"I'm much obliged."

After serving dessert, Marge ushered Tex into the den. She dug into her apron pocket and pulled out a key. "Before we begin, I will ask you to please keep the information I'm about to give you between us. I have no one else I can trust. I suppose I'm at your mercy." She walked over to Harry's desk and opened the file drawer.

"Let's take a look. What we find will not leave this room," Tex said.

Unable to keep her hands from shaking, Marge handed the journals to Tex. An hour passed and then two. After glimpsing through almost half of the entries, he turned to Marge who was seated on a small leather ottoman near the sofa. She was unable to keep her thoughts at bay and was on the verge of tears. "Tex, what do you think?" she blurted.

"Hold on, Marge. Give me a few more minutes." As he read on, it occurred to him Harry was indeed over his head. Having done some jail time himself, he looked directly into her eyes and informed her if what he observed in the journals were true, Harry would be indicted for embezzlement. Marge fell backwards against the sofa.

Tex knew he could not go soft on her. If he did, he would end up helping an old widow instead of himself, and he always came first. Taking her hand in his, he gently pulled her up. Forcing himself to comfort her, he walked her to the stairs. "Look, Marge, this problem can't be solved in one day. You've had a trying time. Suppose we continue this in the morning."

She ignored his request. "Am I responsible for this? If we don't tell anyone and the authorities find out, will I be charged with anything?"

"No one is going to find out, and no, I doubt you can be charged with anything your husband was into. After all, you were not aware of his goings on." That was the second honest thing Tex had conveyed to Marge that day. "Now, relax and get a good night's sleep. Your secrets are safe with me," he lied. Tex watched as she retreated to her bedroom.

Marge woke before sunrise, showered and dressed. She hurried downstairs and into the kitchen to start the percolator. She disliked coffee makers, and it was important to her to start the day with a good cup. Tex turned over in bed. The smell of the fresh brew hit his nostrils. He shielded his eyes from the morning light and for a moment thought he was back in Houston. The aroma beckoned him to jump up and head for the shower. Within forty-five minutes he was standing in Marge's kitchen, showered, shaved, and dressed in a sport shirt and khaki pants. He greeted his hostess with a broad smile.

"Mornin,' Ma'am. I hope you slept well. I sure as heck did."

"I'm so glad you had a good night sleep," Marge responded. She had prepared a breakfast of bacon, scrambled eggs, and toast along with a pot of Columbian coffee. She steadied her hand as she poured the hot liquid into one of the larger mugs which she kept hanging from a shelf under the kitchen window.

Trying not to get caught up in sympathy for the person he was targeting, Tex turned his head and focused on the clock above the window. "I'll chow down; then we can get started. He looked back at Marge. Taking a strip of bacon in one hand, he began waving it in her direction. "Are you ready for some heavy-duty detective work?"

"As soon as you finish that strip of bacon you're shaking at me." Marge chuckled. She felt pacified for the moment.

The sense of relief Marge felt was short lived as they delved deeper into Harry's secret life. It took most of the day for Tex to finish going over the journals. He tried to appear concerned in helping her decide whether or not to inform the authorities. His only interest was to find out what she had encountered in Camwood. Not being able to get to first base with her irritated him. He decided to invite her to dinner that evening in hopes the change of scenery would cause her to talk to him.

Tex insisted on driving Marge's car. "A gentleman never lets the lady drive." They both agreed on Mexican food and found their way to La Cucaracha Grill in downtown Phoenix. Marge knew any restaurant with that name would have to be super clean. Once there, Tex began his interrogation.

"Let's put aside serious talk tonight. Didn't you and your husband take a vacation before he took sick? Why don't you tell me about it."

Marge did not remember speaking to Tex about her trip although she didn't question it. "Yes, we did go away. It was an anniversary gift from the children. Harry seemed on edge before we left, and he didn't want to go. We didn't want to insult them. We enjoyed the company of the other guests—that is, I did. Harry was introverted and not very social. He seemed preoccupied, and I didn't understand why until I searched his office and found those files."

"And there was nothing else—nothing that would concern him?"

"Yes, he didn't get much sleep at the B&B. I thought it was because he was overworked. He was upset about it. Especially one night in particular."

"What night?" Tex's heartbeat accelerated.

"One night—it was late, and everyone had gone to bed. Harry was disturbed by some noise in the parking area below our window. He woke me. He said he heard three cars pull up, one at a time. Several people were talking and carrying on out there. It was after midnight. He asked me to check it out. I was annoyed at him for waking me. After the people left, we tried to get back to sleep."

"What exactly did you hear?" Tex asked. "Did you see who they were?"

"May I take your order?" the waiter interrupted as he took back the Menu's.

Tex's facial muscles stiffened; he ground his teeth. His demeanor went unnoticed. "Why, yes," he uttered. "We'll start off with a spinach and cheese dip, and I'll have the beef fajita."

"I'll have the same, thank you, except make mine chicken," Marge ordered.

"Bring the lady a frozen margarita. I'll have a draft beer," he instructed the waiter. He thought a drink might loosen Marge up a little.

Tex tried to bring the B&B up several times during the evening. Marge was having none of it. She kept changing the subject because she didn't want to talk about the past anymore, which turned his anxiousness into frustration. By the end of the night, he convinced himself it was Harry and Marge who saw what took place in Camwood, and he would report to Joe Balboa in the morning.

They arrived home in time to hear the phone. It was Harry, Jr. on the other end.

"Hello, Mother, what's going on? Are you ok? I've been calling since late afternoon."

"Sorry, Harry. I had a busy day. I did some shopping, and I spent time in the garden and didn't hear the phone." Marge was always forthright with her children. However, this was an exception made to protect Harry Sr. She changed the subject. "Are you enjoying your trip? How are the children?"

"The kids and Lisa are great, and the weather is perfect. You should join us next time. You would love Puerto Rico."

Marge had a flashback of Neva and her description of the island she shared at dinner one night. The ocean never enticed her; she would rather be up in the mountains or shopping at the mall. The memory of Neva made her smile. "When are you due back?"

"Maybe tomorrow night if all goes as planned. We're expecting thunderstorms. We may end up staying an extra day or two. It depends."

Assuming Tex would be gone by then, Marge relaxed. Before going to bed that night, they went through the rest of Harry, Sr.'s personal papers. Marge excused herself and went into the kitchen to make a fresh pot of coffee and some toffee cookies she had made herself earlier in the week. Tex accepted the dessert and instructed her as to how she should conduct herself in the coming weeks.

Marge's face became solemn as Tex dictated her next moves. "I wish I could go back and change a few things. Of course, that's impossible. Harry was a white-collar man, and I had to adjust to his way of life. He was a workaholic, and nothing came before his striving to get ahead. He was afraid to leave the office for any length of time. We did take a few trips from time to time. They were closer to home, always within a few hours driving distance. He hated to go on business trips; he couldn't wait to get back to the office. Now, I realize why......" her voice faded.

"There's already an inside investigation going on in the company," Tex said. "There's no need for you to volunteer any information; they may never link Harry to the missing funds. It was agreed Marge would go on with her life and keep the journals under wraps. If anyone should approach her, either from Filtrec Electronics, or from law enforcement, she was not to let on she was aware of the embezzlement.

The following morning, Marge and Tex said their goodbyes. He insisted on taking a taxi to the airport and arrived at the United Airlines terminal on time for check in and boarding. As he took his seat in coach class, his mind muddled through the events of the past two days. He had scanned through the journals half-heartedly, but he didn't fail to notice the names of the European and Canadian banks that Harry, Sr. had transferred Filtrec's missing funds to.

Tex was not an educated man. He had learned his craft on the streets of Houston. He knew if Harry, Jr. ever confronted him, he had enough on Harry Senior to silence his son

~ CHAPTER TWENTY–SIX ~

Tex slammed down the phone and poured himself a scotch. He had done his job when he filled Joe in on the Burnside's involvement at the Camwood B&B. There would have been no love lost between himself and Marge, yet he was not about to intertwine himself in a murder plot. He didn't want to snuff out the 'ol' broad,' but the lure of the extra cash beckoned him. He decided to give it a day or two before he made his decision.

After mulling it over in his mind, Tex decided he would hire someone for half of his take. *After all, a little money is better than none.* But who? That would take some research as to which cohort to choose—and he knew many. After much thought, he decided on an old jail buddy. He had heard through the grapevine, he had been released a while ago. He knew the smell of new money would be a welcome friend to him.

The apartment was located over a pool hall at the southern end of Houston. Tex hadn't been to that side of town in years, but he never forgot the smell of the dampness and mold the old buildings carried. He gagged when he reached the final landing of the 5th floor walk-up.

He found his way to Apt. 5-B, and with hesitation he leaned against the heavy metal door bolted on the other side with three locks. He pressed hard on the bell. It took half a minute for the barrier to swing open, and Tex was face to face with a fellow ex-con.

"If it isn't my old roommate," Frank 'Mo' Digbey moved aside to let his visitor pass. He smiled at Tex, exposing a set of neglected teeth, some missing—most rotted.

Mo, as he was known, was small in stature and underweight. He had the appearance he couldn't hurt a fly. He had served 25 years of a life sentence in federal prison for aiding and abetting in the robbery and murder of a gas station attendant. He was released two years earlier. Although he hadn't pulled the trigger, he was charged with the same felony. Hunted down for many months, the authorities had finally caught up with him through a snitch who knew where he was holding out. He served his time and hoped to be paroled one day. When that day finally came, he vowed to walk a straight line. Then Tex called.

Tex sensed Mo would be hard up for cash. If his timing was right, he would take the bait

"Hey old Buddy" Tex said. "It's been a while." Both men shook hands.

Mo motioned to Tex, "Have a seat. Welcome to my palace."

Tex didn't have to check out his surroundings a second time. He took it all in with his first glance around the two-room flat. *How sad, he thought, this bird has gone nowhere since he left his cage.*

"What brings you this way, Tex? I know this isn't a social call," Mo asked.

"To be honest with you, it isn't, and I can see by the looks of things you could use a little dough about now."

"Depends on what you're lookin' at."

Struggling to get the words out, Tex whispered, "I need a job done, Mo, if you know what I mean."

"If you're asking me what I think you are, the answer is no." Mo jumped up and began to pace. "Do you think after spending 25 years in the clinker, I'm gonna risk a return visit? You're a few beers short of a six pack, Buddy."

Tex also stood. He grabbed Mo's arm and held tight. "Hear me out. That's all I ask. The take is high, fifty grand on your end," he lied. "How about I give you a week to decide. Take this." He handed Mo his calling card. "If you're interested, give me a call. I'll find my way out of this flea bag myself. All I need to do is turn around and open the door."

Mo slumped down on the musty brown sofa. Making a loud noise as they hit the hard surface, several moth balls slid from one of the cushions and rolled down onto the torn linoleum floor toward the kitchen. The sound reminded him of how poor he was. The smell of camphor filled his nostrils. He placed his hands over his face and rocked back and forth. He had to think. He knew this would be a way out of the hell hole he inhabited.

It was a rainy afternoon, as bleak as his thoughts, when Mo picked up the phone and dialed Tex's number. After much soul searching, he had decided his future was damned. He knew if he did do the job, he would have to do it clean and leave no traces of evidence that would point his way. He didn't want to go back to the glass house, as his cellmates called it, but there was nothing he could look forward to without the means he needed to survive. Pulling the card Tex had given him from his pocket, he dialed his number.

"Tex, is that you?"

"Yea, it's me. That you, Mo?"

"Yeah, listen. I've been thinking. This must be done in such a way that nothing, and I mean nothing, can be traced back to me. You hear? You've never contacted me or even heard my name mentioned—deal?"

"Deal. There's a motel right off 45 about half a mile from Hobby Airport. It has a truckers' area in the back. Meet me there at 10 p.m." No other words were spoken.

~ CHAPTER TWENTY-SEVEN ~

Knowing most of the staff would be gone, Detective Chen Young walked into Sergeant Larry O'Donnell's office on a Friday evening. Since his encounter with Niki at the country club, Chen had spent a lot of time soul searching and praying. He made up his mind to tell the truth. Expecting to see his superior leaning back in his chair, feet upon the desk, phone to his ear, he entered the office and found his seat empty and no one in sight. "Maybe it's the wrong move, or my timing is off," Chen mumbled. He removed a handkerchief from the back pocket of his jeans and began to dab the salty liquid that had eased down the side of his face onto his cheek. As he turned around to leave, he came face to face with Larry. He had been standing behind him for several seconds and watching his every move.

It was obvious to Chen that Larry sensed something was amiss. This motivated him to speak. He wanted nothing better than to get this night over with. "Hello, Sarge, is it too late, or can I take some of your time?"

"Time is all I have," the sergeant responded. "My wife is away with the kids, and believe it or not, I'd rather be here then go home to an empty house. What brings you my way? Got anything for me, Chen?" His eyes narrowed as he spoke.

"Yes, I do. Do you mind if I sit?"

"Be my guest. I'm all ears." Larry took a seat across from Chen's. "You haven't given me anything in weeks," he chided, unaware the information he was about to hear would blow the lid off his own internal investigation.

Chen sat there for almost an hour, revealing the details of how he got involved with Joe Balboa and Brian White. He felt Marge Bernside may be in danger since he had led Joe into believing Niki had nothing to do with witnessing what happened in Camwood. His confession was thorough—he left nothing out, including his conversion to Christianity. The sergeant listened intently, his face showing no signs of shock or disappointment in his fellow officer, but the adrenaline had kicked in.

When Chen finished speaking, he sucked in the stale air the room offered and waited for the inevitable. He was sure he would be handcuffed and arrested. He believed he would be prosecuted for his crimes—the crime of turning his head when he should have reported what he knew, the crime of not making arrests to stop the drug trafficking, and finally, the crime of becoming one of them. Not to mention the money he had made and spent—the dirty money, the cash Joe was enjoying at this very moment. There was no excuse for any of it. Chen knew his career was over, and he must face the consequences of his actions.

Larry sat there for at least five minutes and said nothing. Then he spoke. "I knew there was something going on in the department for a while. I couldn't put my finger on it." He leaned over his desk, their noses nearly touched. "I have suspected Balboa of going over to the other side. You, being vulnerable, were sucked into this whirlwind of crime." There was silence once more. Larry was in deep thought, but he never took his eyes off Chen. "How about I cut you a deal? What if you continue as if nothing has happened until we have enough on these bozos to convict them. We need evidence. I'm sure we can promise you immunity from prosecution and your safety if you work with us."

Chen was speechless and overwhelmed with the thought God loved him that much to give him another chance at life. He was humbled. "I told Joe I wanted out after I had accepted Christ into my life," he responded. "He didn't take it too well. I could never go on living like I was. My hands are dirty, I have blood on my hands, and I want to be clean. I've confessed to my Lord, and I'm confessing to you."

"What blood?" The Sergeant said. "You didn't kill anyone. You made some bad choices. The ball's in your court. You have my word this conversation will not leave this office until I nail those dogs and they never see freedom again."

"I have put the Bernside woman in jeopardy. If I work with you, we have to act fast. I have to convince Joe I want in again," Chen said.

It was obvious to Larry that Chen was convicted of his wrongdoing. "You're all we have Chen. The drugs are long gone. I want you to arrange one more transaction so we can apprehend them. You won't be implicated. As far as the Bernside woman, I'll contact Phoenix and see what they can do to protect her. Unless we have evidence that her life is in danger, there is not much they can do about it. That's where you come in. If you arrange to continue with the trafficking, we can wire you up and tap Balboa's phones at the same time. We'll have to go through the proper channels to do that. Hopefully we can get him on both charges. We need him on tape."

Chen rose from his seat and grasped Larry's hand. He promised to be in touch with him within the week. As he left the building, he held tight to the handrail and descended the flight of steps to the street. His vision was blurred from the grateful tears that would not stop flowing. He was not ashamed to cry.

~ CHAPTER TWENTY-EIGHT ~

It took several days for Neva to recuperate from her garden mishap. Alma didn't leave her side. She remained with her friend far into the night and adhered to all the instructions Doctor Ottorro had given her. Having suffered a concussion, Neva had developed several of the symptoms Alma had been instructed to look for, and after the confusion had cleared up, Neva was able to describe what happened to her before she passed out. When she complained of a severe headache, it convinced Alma to stay a few nights longer. Under the doctor's orders, she applied cool compresses intermittently until the large lump on her temple subsided.

Alma knew God's timing was perfect. She was grateful she was at home the day of Neva's accident. She was aware God's plans were different from hers, and she didn't question why she had gotten up two hours late and missed her appointment with the church board.

During one of their chats together, Neva confided in Alma about the stranger that befriended her on the plane. "A man they called Tex," she said. Although she didn't go into every detail of their encounter, she did explain how she had taken a liking to him in a motherly sort of way. "He was respectful," she said, "but he did ask a lot of questions. I don't know why he'd be so interested in the life of an old woman, but he seemed sincere." Her expression changed. "I stopped hearing from him. It's like he walked off the face of the earth."

Alma listened to the narration and smiled. "Dear, that's what happens when you choose someone forty years younger than yourself. I believe it's called, 'robbing the cradle.' Both women laughed.

Neva hadn't laughed in a long time. It was a childish laugh, and it felt good. She went on with her saga. "All kidding aside, there was something mysterious about Tex. He was respectful, I grant you, and thoughtful. He even took me out to dinner. He seemed interested in the island and how Martin and I got started in the tobacco industry. Of course, there wasn't enough time to go through all the details then. That's what's puzzling me. Since he was alone with no friends in San Juan, he told me we would have many other nights when I could share my story with him. I'm concerned something has happened to my new friend. I had expected him to call the day I fell in the garden."

"There you go Neva, always thinking the worst," Alma scolded. "Give the man a little space, will you? Maybe he's not looking for your nurturing spirit. He may have a mother or a wife somewhere. Your instincts have taken over your good sense. He was passing the time while visiting the island. If he wanted you to contact him, he would have given you his number."

"He did," Neva responded. "I didn't want to impose on his schedule, so I didn't call him. She leaned over and patted Alma's hand. "You are right, my dear." She forced a smile. "I'll leave him in God's Hands for now, and if he does contact me again, I'll consider it a gift."

~ CHAPTER TWENTY-NINE ~

Fall erupted with an array of magentas, reds, and yellows. Jack was busy revamping the window display at his photography studio. He and Anne had been married for several weeks, and life was good. Young Sean had completed his final high school semester and was preparing to enter college. He had been offered a scholarship to several different universities but chose to attend a private college nestled in the mountains of New England's northwest.

The rolling hills and brick facades with their arched porticos, and the historical buildings, in Greek Revival, with their white columns topped with scroll like designs, stood majestically in the sunlight and appealed to Sean." The library is in there." He pointed to the ivy-covered hall with its prominent dormers. It's being renovated. They've added a huge computer lab, some study rooms with the latest high-tech equipment, and a cafe," he explained proudly.

"And what's that building?" Anne pointed to a tall brick building covered in vines with a turret-like structure attached to it.

"Oh, that's the administration building. The president's office is on the third floor. The dean's office is also there."

Anne had accompanied Sean to the college once before during the summer. They had visited the shops and museums and attended the Theatre Festival. Helping Sean get a feel of dorm life resulted in a special bond long overdue. She was a good listener, at least she thought she was, and so she gave advice only when asked. Sean trusted her opinions on how to dress and style his hair and finally asked advice on how to date a co-ed. "Traditions have changed through the years, Sean," she said. "You must show respect to someone you choose to date. Open the car door for her, don't use bad language, and if you promise to call later on in the week, do so. The most important advice I can give you is don't talk negative about her to the other guys if you don't like her. You need not date her again. It's that simple."

"How do I break the relationship?" Sean had asked.

"There are ways, Sean. That's another story. When you get to that point, let us know. I'm sure your dad could give you some pointers."

As they continued their tour, Anne glanced at her watch and frowned. "It's getting late, Sean. We should head back. It will take hours, and I would like to get home before midnight."

"I hope you liked what you saw today," Sean said. "It's important to me that you and dad approve of the college I chose."

"Sean, we are proud of you," Anne said, with a twinkle in her eye. "We knew you would make the right decision. If you keep your head on straight and not compromise yourself in any way..."

"What do you mean?" Sean interrupted.

"I mean if someone is doing something that goes against your ethics, don't compromise to fit in." Anne smiled, "Be yourself, Sean. That's all." They headed for the highway.

It was after one a.m., when Anne pulled into the driveway. Sean had been dosing off and on in the front seat.

"Sean, we're home," Anne said softly.

Sean opened his eyes and glanced at the clock on the dashboard. "Does that time say what I think is says? He stepped out of the car and turned to Anne. "Thanks for today—I mean driving so far and all."

"You're welcome, Sean. I'll look forward to our next trip when I see you settled in your dorm."

Sean jumped out of the car and hurried to his room. Jack who had been waiting for them was sitting on the sofa when he got a glimpse of

Sean charging up the stairs.

"Wait, Son, how was your day?"

"Sorry, Dad. I didn't see you," Sean answered. "I'm going to bed—I'm beat. I'll tell you about it in the morning."

Anne who was following close behind laughed. "It's been quite a day," she said. "I'm sure he'll get it all in tomorrow."

Jack, too, was tired. He had worked all day on the new display. It took several hours to set up the photos he had enlarged. He had chosen some of his best images, enhanced them, and with the help of the Artisan Frame Store, had each one matted and framed to perfection. The Artisan had worked with Jack for many years. Their expertise was framing in the Baroque and Rococo styles and turning plain images into masterpieces. They also worked with simpler designs but were known for their opulence. Jack had mounted several of his framed black and white photos on easels of different heights. Each frame complimented its subject. Family photos were framed in a simpler style while wedding or scenic photos were surrounded by thick wooden carvings that had been painted over in 24 karat gold leaf. Several of the images had a frame within a frame, Victorian style, adding to their grandeur.

Feeling both had accomplished something, Jack and Anne sat on the sofa and filled each other in. "The display is finished," Jack said. "It looks good. Sorry, I couldn't go with you guys today. I know it was a lot on you, Anne, but it had to be completed for the fall season. You know my busiest time is upon me with school pictures, weddings, and fall festivals on the horizon."

Anne smiled, "We had a good time. Every time we plan something alone, I get to know Sean a little better."

Jack was relieved Sean and Anne were getting along. It was one of his main concerns. His son had been without a mother for so long, and his acceptance of Anne would determine if the family would make it through the tough times. As the couple retired to their room for the night, Anne decided to wait until Sean left for college to tell Jack she was carrying their first child.

~ CHAPTER THIRTY ~

Niki missed her talks with Chen, but she knew in her heart she was doing the right thing. Leaving him to the Lord and not interfering with God's plan for their lives was hard but necessary. Chen was being faithful. He had cooperated with Sergeant O'Donnell and wanted Niki to know he was given another chance at life but kept his promise not to contact her.

A light shower fell and accelerated into a torrential downpour. It was late Friday afternoon. Niki gazed out of her bedroom window and watched the rain as it cascaded over the street and lawns. It reminded her of God's majesty and power. The parched ground, so in need of moisture, was being touched by His Hand. *These things go unnoticed by many. A world occupied with so many concerns it is unable to see the small miracles that are bypassed without a thought.*

Deciding not to spend the remainder of the day brooding, she showered and dressed, had a quick bite, and hopped into her car. She had made a mental note at the beginning of the week to stop at Bigelow's and buy a small gift for each member of her prayer group. She would present the gifts at the next meeting along with a message telling them how she sees and appreciates each one as God does.

Niki enjoyed shopping at Bigelow's. There was a bookstore located in the rear of the building that housed a cafe called Johnny's. Niki had gone to high school with the owner, and they remained fast friends. She decided she would buy several gifts, check out the latest novels, stop for a coffee, and return home before the roads became flooded. After an hour of browsing, she walked to the religious book section. To her delight, she noticed the book she had been longing to buy had been released, and a copy of it was standing erect on top of a display. She had seen the author on a local morning TV show and was impressed with his concept of Bible prophecy. She decided she would purchase the volume for a friend who had been questioning her on the subject. As she reached for the book, a hand covered her hand and gently pulled her around. She found herself staring into the face of Chen Young, a face that had aged a bit despite his young years. She stammered unable to hide her emotions. "Oh, my Lord, you frightened me, Chen. How are you?"

"I see you are about to buy the book I came here for. How are you, Nicole?" He had never called her by that name before. She recognized the pain in his voice.

"I'm glad to see you, Chen. How have you been?"

"Better than ever."

Niki could see tears in Chen's eyes, yet there was a peace about him.

"Would you consider having a cup of coffee with me tonight?" Chen asked. "I know we have agreed not to see each other, but so much has taken place in the last few weeks. Please let me share it with you. You will be surprised."

"I'm happy for you, but there hasn't been enough time for you to get your life back on track. We need more time. It was wonderful to see you tonight. I need to go. It may be a monsoon out there by now."

Niki picked up a second copy of the book and turned to walk away. Chen grabbed her arm and once again swung her around to face him. "Nik, I'm begging you. Please hear me out this one time. You won't be disappointed. I promise."

There was silence. Then Niki answered. Her tone was soft but firm. "I will consider it on one condition—we don't mention our relation-ship even once."

As they sat in the cafe, Chen related to Niki everything that had taken place since he last saw her. "It has been weeks since we last spoke. Since that time, my life has taken a complete turn in the right direction. God has given me a second chance. I should be in jail right now, but the Lord had other plans for me. The night I went to see Sergeant O'Donnell was the turning point. I knew God existed, but I wasn't sure He'd be interested in someone like me. I knew I had to tell the truth. I heard once the truth always wins, so I decided to trust in Him alone. I know He's a just Judge, and I was willing to take whatever consequences I would reap. The sergeant listened as I told him everything that took place, and he gave me another opportunity to set my life straight."

Niki was speechless. She knew what she was hearing was an act of God. Then she spoke. "When we go off on our own, without the Lord's direction, we sometimes pay a great price. The Lord is a just God, yes, but there are times He makes an exception. He sees the potential in someone and knows that with his repentance He can use that person for His greater glory. Look at the Apostle Paul. He was a persecutor of Christians. He went on to be one of the greatest evangelists of all time." She searched his eyes to see if he understood. "I heard a story once about a man on death row who was exonerated of his death sentence. His mother had tried to drown him at birth. He felt he was worthless and had no purpose. He ended up in jail, and he began to read God's Word. He developed a relationship with Christ. He was scrubbing the floor one day, and the Lord spoke to him. He heard God's voice say the next person to walk by him would set him free of that sentence. The warden had a dream the night before. In that dream God told him the person he would pass by in the corridor should be considered for a reduced sentence." Chen, leaned in with anticipation." What happened?"

"It's a story like yours in a way. In time he was set free. But that was freedom from incarceration of his body. Jesus had already set him free from the imprisonment of his soul. He became a Pastor."

The testimony uplifted Chen. It gave him the courage to ask, "Niki, I want you to know I, too, have been faithful to Him. I've sought counseling, and I'm attending a Bible study. I've joined a Bible believing church, and I haven't missed a Sunday. Would you consider going out with me again?"

"It's too soon. You've been a Christian for how long, two months? I must see fruit. I have to be sure of a definite change."

"Would you consider meeting me at church. I do need support, and knowing you are sitting beside me will encourage me. I would like for you to meet my pastor."

Niki's face remained expressionless. She was silent for nearly a minute. It seemed to Chen as if an hour had passed. "I will meet with you on Sunday. We will take it one Sunday at a time."

Another exoneration—another redemptive moment. He didn't deserve it, he knew, but he jumped at the proposal of seeing her once a week. He was hopeful the week would turn to days, and the days would turn into a lifetime.

Sarah was concerned. It was past 10 p.m., and the downpour hadn't ceased. She could hear the rush of water flowing through the drainpipes on both sides of the house. She knew Niki was going to Bigelow's to do some shopping. She didn't expect her to be this late. *This is nothing short of a hurricane*. She repeated aloud the words of Psalm 91. "He who dwells in the shelter of the Most High will rest in the shadow of the Almighty. I will say of the Lord, He is my refuge and my fortress, my God in whom I trust." As she prayed, a calming peace came over her. No longer overwhelmed, she retrieved her novel and read for at least another hour before she heard the sound of the front door open.

"Niki, is that you?"

"Who else would it be, Mom? Expecting anyone?"

"No, of course not, what kept you so long? I was worried."

"I ran into an old friend and we got to talking."

Niki ran up the steps two at a time to avoid further conversation. She threw her packages on the bed and undressed. She decided she would wait before telling her mother of her encounter with Chen. She wanted to be sure there was a definite change in him and figured only time would tell. "I have a lot of praying to do," Niki said aloud, "a lot of praying."

~ CHAPTER THIRTY-ONE ~

Mo Digbey paced as he waited for Tex to arrive. The truckers' parking area was enveloped in a blanket of fog. It was a few minutes passed 10 p.m., and the dark of night along with the thick mist that surrounded Mo made him feel secure. It wasn't until half past ten he heard footsteps approaching. The glow of his cigarette got brighter. He took one last drag and tossed its remains on the tarred pavement. He stepped on it with a vengeance as Tex approached him—his hand extended.

"You're not crashing on me, are you?" Tex felt the vibration in Mo's hand.

"I'm here, aren't I? Give me the details. Let's get this over with."

A smidgen of guilt gnawed at Tex. He dug into his jacket pocket and pulled out a sealed and folded brown manila envelope. He opened it and handed Mo prepared outlines of what was to take place the following week which included a makeshift map Tex had drawn himself. The instructions were printed in big bold letters as if his accomplice had just learned to read. "Here's her name and address, and here's the time she's usually alone."

"I'm listening." The tremor in Mo's left hand grew stronger.

"You can easily break into the house. You're an expert in that category." His smile was short lived. "Rely on your expertise."

The sound of rushing traffic from the highway added to Mo's uneasiness. He took the papers, folded them in half, and stuffed them in his front shirt pocket.

"Don't mess up, Brother. There's no room for error here."

Mo nodded. The lights of an approaching truck blinded them for a moment. They terminated their exchange without a handshake and walked in opposite directions.

It was close to midnight, when Mo turned the latch key to his apartment and stepped inside. He could feel the sweat dripping off his forehead half-hidden under his faded houndstooth cap. He pulled out a handkerchief from the back pocket of his jeans and began to dab his brow. Was he capable of murder? He didn't know. Although he was an accessory to one, he knew he would have to be desperate to commit one himself. He would have to talk himself into the fact he was desperate—he wasn't sure.

Interrupted by the ring of the phone, Mo dashed into the kitchen and grabbed the receiver. *It's Tex, and he's going to tell me to forget the plan.* "Hello." Silence followed. "Who is this?"

A familiar voice could be heard on the other end. "Hey, Mo, that you? I heard you were out and living in town. It's your old cell mate Louie."

"Hey, Lou, how have you been—when did you get out?"

"A few months ago. I didn't know you were here in town until I heard it from the grapevine." Lou Parisi laughed as if he had told a bad joke. "Is it too late to call?"

"Now what gives you that idea? What've you been up to, Lou?"

"Staying straight, but it's not easy." Lou's voice sounded like he had been around much longer than his forty-five years. "How about we get together for a beer, Mo, for old time's sake? Huh?"

"Sorry, I want to forget old times. Know what I mean?"

"How about we get together for a beer period?"

Mo could hear Lou's fragile laugh. He placed the phone down and grabbed a cigarette. Biding him a fraction of time, he sucked in the smoke and slowly let it out. "Listen, Lou, I got a lot going on. Leave me your number, and I'll get back to you. Maybe we can meet in a week or two."

After jotting down Lou's number, Mo returned to the couch and opened the papers Tex had given him. In large print he read the name and address of the woman in Phoenix, the best time to find her home alone, and the name and address of the pawn shop where he was to pick up the weapon along with instructions on where to discard it after the job was done. Tex had stressed to Mo he was never to contact him again and the money he earned would be sent to him by courier. He ended his instructions with the words: YOU ARE ON YOUR OWN.

Lucy Bella Donna

~ CHAPTER THIRTY-TWO ~

Niki could not remember a Saturday it didn't rain. She welcomed the sun's rays that poured through the lace panels of her bedroom window. She began to hum one of her favorite old-time gospel tunes and flitted around the room. She picked up a blouse here and a sweater and scarf there and placed each one in the hamper she kept hidden in her walk-in closet. The melody soon turned to lyrics as her crystal-clear voice sang out. Before the song ended, her bedroom floor was intact.

Between work and church services, Niki hadn't had enough time to shop for something special to wear to her lunch date with Chen. She took out a plain beige pencil skirt from her closet and paired it with a black, short sleeved, turtleneck sweater. Holding her choice up and satisfied with the image in the mirror, she placed the items gently on her bed and proceeded to take a shower and blow dry her hair.

Since that stormy night encounter with Chen at Bigelow's, Niki had attended two church services with him. After each service, they agreed to go their separate ways. Chen finally got the courage to invite her to lunch, and Niki accepted. She believed he had turned his life around, and she was willing to remain a friend and encourage him in his walk with Christ. They would meet at Chasins at two p.m.

Chen stared at his watch in intervals. He had never known Niki to be late. *Could she have changed her mind?* He began to pray silently. *Lord, if you give me another chance, I will not blow it again.* Niki had taught him if you pray in your prayer closet, that is, in your mind, where no one but God can hear, you can overcome the deceitful cunnings of the enemy. Several minutes passed. When he raised his eyes, he saw a slim silhouette descending the steps into the dining room. *How beautiful she looks,* he thought, as he rose from his chair to greet her.

The luncheon went better than they had expected. Chen promised Niki he would keep the conversation light and not discuss their past relationship. Niki managed to keep her side of the bargain. Chen was unable to hide his feelings.

"Niki, things have gone exceedingly well for me these past few weeks. The Lord has given me another chance at life. I've been faithful to my promises to Him. The sarge has also given me another chance. If I continue to follow Christ, to live for Him, as I have been, would you consider seeing me on a regular basis? I need an incentive to keep going."

"The only incentive you need Chen is Jesus. He's the glue to keep things in perspective. Her tone remained serious, "I do see you have been consistent."

"Is that a yes?"

"Yes, it's a yes. I will see you after church if you like each Sunday. We could spend that time together and see how things go."

Chen was ecstatic. Keeping with a promise he made to himself, he did not mention he had arranged a meeting with Joe at the request of Sergeant O'Donnell. Niki and Sarah had been targeted as suspects of Joe Balboa, and Chen's objective was to wipe their names off his slate. He had succeeded. Niki hadn't a clue they were no longer on Joe's list or that they were ever on his list to begin with.

~ CHAPTER THIRTY-THREE ~

Mo went into his usual ritual when stressed. The residents on the lower floor were used to his pacing, which could last for hours, and stopped complaining. Hearing from his old cell mate had jolted him. He promised himself once out of prison he would distance himself from any reminders of the past, but his mind would not rest. The temptation to involve Lou was becoming too great. He reached for the phone several times that afternoon but never did make the call. He needed help if he was going to get the job done, and he knew if anyone was capable of killing without remorse, it was this hit man.

Lou Parisi had served his time. He managed to stay out of serious trouble for the twenty-plus years he had served in the system. Although he had killed many times before, he was only convicted once for the murder of a drug dealer who had honed in on his territory.

Lou had been losing deals and wanted this pusher out of the way. He arranged to meet him at a popular hangout that was frequented by dealers and addicts in downtown Houston. The victim never got out of his car. He was gunned down mercilessly, gangland style. Lou was indeed responsible for the killing, but he wasn't convicted right away. He got rid of the evidence by having the gun discarded in the middle of a lake over 100 miles away from the crime scene until it was discovered by a diver commissioned to look for a missing woman. The gun was traced back to him, and he was sentenced by a Judge to serve 30 years to life with the possibility of parole if he would take a plea bargain as an informant. He agreed to co-operate with the law. He sang out loud and clear, giving names, locations, and numbers, which were traced and recorded. His behavior while incarcerated was commendable enough to convince the parole board he was ready for a hearing. He never envisioned what life would be like once out of confinement. Unable to get work, he ended up washing dishes, off the books, in a roach infested noodle house in Houston's Chinatown.

Mo picked up his pack of unfiltered cigarettes from the sofa. He pulled one, lit it, and blew smoke rings into the darkness. He watched the circles dissipate into the air until they vanished. Entering the kitchen, he reached for the phone and dialed the number he had scribbled down earlier.

"This is Lin Lin's Noodle House," sang the shrilled voice. "Would you like to order?"

"I'm looking for Lou Parisi."

"Aaaah, Mr. Lou's in the back working. Is it an emergency?"

"Have him call me," Mo left his name and number.

It took another day before Lou contacted him. Moe explained to him what he had to say could not be said on the phone. "Meet me downtown at the Imperial Diner on Friday night at nine. Make sure you are not followed and come alone."

"What's this all about?" Lou asked.

"I'll explain on Friday. Just be there."

Mo sat in a booth situated in the back of the diner near the rest rooms. He sat there for twenty minutes, facing the entrance door. One wouldn't guess by observing him he was about to ask someone to commit a murder. He motioned to the waitress who approached him smiling and carrying a menu.

"I'll have some water for now," Mo said. "I'm expecting a friend." The waitress responded with a dirty look she thought he deserved. Noticing his appearance, she didn't expect his friend to look any better and thought the order wouldn't go beyond two coffees. After waiting another fifteen minutes, Lou came meandering through the door.

"Ok, so you dragged me to this hash house," Lou walked up to Mo's table and sat. "What's the big secret?"

Mo leaned across the table. "I've been offered a job, Lou," he whispered. Lots of cash, enough for both of us to live on pretty good. Things aren't going so great. You know how it is when you leave the big house. But this is a huge one, and I need the help. I'm willing to split fifty-fifty."

"Listen, I paid my dues to society, and I'm not about to return for an extended visit," Lou said, meeting him half-way.

Mo looked around before speaking. He lowered his tone. I'm supposed to knock off some old broad in Phoenix."

Lou's droopy eyes narrowed. "Are you crazy, Buddy, I've been clean since I'm out, and I intend to stay that way."

Ignoring the comment, Mo continued. "To start 10k, and another ten when the job is done."

"And what's in it for you?" Lou asked.

"Half of the take."

Lou thought for about half a minute, before he responded. "Who's pulling the trigger?" His voice barely audible.

"You, of course."

"You get half of the take and expect me to split that, and I'm doing the dirty work. You're one sick cow if you think I wouldn't take more than you. I want seventy percent of your take, nothing less, and I want to think it over first."

Lou got up, threw a dollar on the table, and walked away. There was no response from Mo as he watched his fellow inmate go through the exit door and disappear into the night.

It took a little longer than a week for Lou to contact Mo. He had thought long and hard about his offer and had reached his decision several days after they had their meeting at the Imperial Diner. He took extra time. He hoped Mo would cave and agree to give him what he had asked for.

Mo still had a conscience about killing. His thinking was if you didn't pull the trigger, you were less guilty. He hadn't learned anything from his last conviction of aiding and abetting, but Lou's morals had left him a long time ago. The only thing Lou was concerned about was getting caught. He was proud of the fact he had managed to stay straight the few months he was out. He was living at the mercy of his Great Aunt Thelma, now in her nineties. He made pennies at the Noodle House, enough to help his aunt with one of the utilities — sometimes two, but for the most part he paid the remainder of the bills with her Social Security check and left a little for himself.

Mo settled down for a nap, after his usual midday visit to place his bets in town and drifted off. He always kept the room dark even in daylight. His dreams, when he remembered them, haunted him, and this one was no exception. It was interrupted with gratitude when he heard the phone resonating off the wall. He groped his way into the kitchen and grabbed the receiver.

"Yeah," Mo sounded like a canyon tree frog.

"It's me, Lou."

"Yeah, what's happening?"

"Meet me at the Rec Center on Saturday. I'll explain then."

"What time?"

"One — is one good?"

"You got it."

The two men hung up simultaneously. Mo felt the moisture build up on his forehead. He lifted his right arm and brushed his shirt sleeve across his brow. *What if Tex knew I was hiring someone else to do the job?* Then reasoned, *what's it to him how it gets done. He won't find out anyway.*

It was open house for seniors at the Rec Center. This fall day was hotter than usual, and Mo was enjoying the air-conditioned lobby. He spotted Lou rushing through the revolving glass door and heading for the reception area. They had both decided to take the metro rail exiting at Canterberry Street. Lou missed the 12:20 p.m. train and arrived late which gave his friend extra time to torture his mind.

Lou trusted Mo to a degree, but his trust had a limit. He had the day planned out. They would mingle in with the old folks, meander about, watch a few demonstrations, and perhaps take in a class or two. He was also hoping to take advantage of the pantries, stocked with canned goods, and the used clothing they offered. And talk. They had to talk.

As they walked around the aquatic area on the first floor, they listened as the instructors explained the importance of mastering your swimming skills and building confidence in the water plus the wide range of options offered to students with an emphasis on first time swimmers. Lou laughed. "When did you last have a swimming lesson, Mo?"

"Never," Mo grinned, showing the gaps between his teeth.

They continued their tour of the building and ambled through the gym, passed a sauna, and ended up in the locker room. Finding they were alone, Mo spoke first."Tex called me today. He arranged for my trip to Phoenix on Thursday. He reserved a first class, round trip ticket. Can you beat that? The Phoenix woman must have sent it to him for a return trip. Part of the perks I guess. I had the tickets switched to two coach seats. We leave Thursday. Be at the airport at eleven. I'll meet you at the United Terminal."

"What happens when we get there?" Lou asked.

"He said not to take a cab. He arranged for me to pick up a car at Sky Harbor."

It was after three p.m. when their plane touched down in Phoenix. Mo felt queasy. A feeling of impending doom enveloped him. His throat became tight, his breaths short. He was in one of his panic modes but there was no time to pace. He groped for his duffle bag and the two men hurried to the car center to confirm the reservation.

With the car rental out of the way, Lou was still in limbo.

He looked at Mo. "What's next?"

"Tex told me to pick up the weapon at a pawn shop," Mo said, "and throw it in some lake when I'm done. The owner is a personal buddy, so no background check." He handed Lou two crumpled up pieces of paper. "Here's the pawn shop, and here's the location of the lake," pointing to the make shift map Tex had scribbled out. "It's about 60 miles from the old lady's house."

Lou seemed satisfied with the plan. He pressed the button on the dashboard, and country music came roaring out of the speakers. He smiled as he lay his head against the headrest. The song was familiar and he began to hum in his usual baritone voice, interjecting a word here and there. Mo laughed.

The pawn shop was about three miles from the airport. Lou waited in the car. In a matter of minutes Mo returned, carrying a Glock semi-automatic in a paper bag. The ammunition was in a small box he removed from his jacket pocket and handed to Lou. He placed the weapon in the backpack he had brought with him and threw it into the duffle bag. Reality set in. Lou's hands began to vibrate. He took the box and placed it next to him on the passenger seat. He turned up the A/C, leaned back, and closed his eyes.

Marge had just finished a hot bath. She slipped into a pair of light cotton pajamas and curled up in her favorite chair. She shut her eyes for a moment and thought back on the events of the day. She had met Jennifer for lunch, hoping to settle some of Harry Sr.'s financial statements. She was depending on her son to help get things under control. She had been bombarded with phone calls from creditors since Harry's passing, and it seemed although her husband was stashing it away in foreign banks, he left a multitude of unpaid bills to his wife. She was hoping her son could reach a compromise with the lenders. Remembering she had not locked up the house properly for the night, Marge placed her novel on the oval oak table under her bedroom's bay window and descended the stairs toward the kitchen. Setting the alarm in the hallway, she entered the kitchen and closed the lights. She proceeded through the other rooms on the main level and repeated the ritual.

Harry Jr. had arranged for a surveillance system to be set up for Marge after his father's death. Although she was grateful, she had continued her habit of keeping most of the lights on until she went to bed. As she entered the living area, she began to shut one of the five lamps that illuminated the room. She reminisced about how she and Harry bought them together and how they argued over each one. She was never included in making the bigger decisions. She stood her ground on the smaller ones. Everything of importance had to be Harry's way, and after time it made no difference to her. She was used to his control and succumbed to it.

Mo and Lou planned their arrival after dark. They parked half a block away from Marge's home and walked the rest of the way, circling around toward the backyard. Noticing the lights were still on, they situated themselves behind the bushes on the side of the house facing the south windows. The area was surrounded by variegated shade trees and a six-foot cedar fence with a lattice top that lined the back and sides of the house. They were secure. They would go unnoticed.

Lou opened the duffle bag and removed the backpack Mo had placed inside. He took out the Glock, checked the rounds, and placed the magazine into its chamber, as Mo watched.

Mo's entire body trembled, and his face turned to chalk. "Good thing you ain't pulling the trigger," Lou mocked. "It's bedtime. She should be shutting down the lights soon."

The two men crouched like a pair of leopards waiting to spring on their prey. Their shadows formed silhouettes on the white clapboard siding. Along with the image of the Glock placed securely in Lou's hand, it created the illusion of an old black and white whodunit from the silent era.

Marge entered the den and went straight to Harry's desk. She cleared off some of the papers Harry, Jr. had left and placed them in the top drawer. She moved about closing several of the lights and walked to the windows. Mo recognized Marge from the description Tex had given him. He whispered, "That's her."

Now taking on the form of two demons about to snatch away the soul of the innocent, the perpetrators silhouettes remained on the siding. Lou lifted the Glock, and with his forefinger he seized hold of the trigger, aiming directly at his target.

Marge walked over to the oak barristers cabinet in front of the windows and leaned forward to lower the blinds. The blast echoed in the night air and resounded through the neighboring streets. Simultaneously the security alarm in the hallway did its job. Second story lights illuminated as groggy sleepers ran to their windows. The professional hit man forgot to check out the alarm's wiring system. The projectile tore through the glass pane and struck Marge in the lower right part of her skull. Her fingers caught a cord as she fell to the floor and pulled one blind down with her.

The men had hit their mark. Mo grabbed the Glock from Lou. He shoved the weapon into the duffle bag along with the backpack and darted toward the street. Having fallen backwards with the blast, Lou, still in shock, remained on the ground for half a minute. He managed to pull himself up and follow in his cohort's footsteps. As the felons raced toward the car, they were both thinking the same thought. *If a neighbor had witnessed the shooting, their days of freedom would be over.*

Mo reached the car first. Unable to control his hand, it took him half a minute to start the engine. Lou, following close behind, jumped into the passenger seat. He never had a chance to close the door. The car took off, tearing through the streets with the headlights off. Once they approached the Interstate, Mo turned the headlights on and headed in the direction of the airport.

"Aren't you forgetting something? Besides the silencer you were supposed to get me," Lou asked.

"What are you talking about?" Mo ignored the dig.

"The lake—aren't we supposed to drop the Glock in a lake somewhere?"

Shaken, Mo headed for the nearest exit ramp and pulled the car over to the side. He took out the crumpled map from his pocket and studied the area of the lake. "It must be a deserted area, or Tex wouldn't have suggested it," he said.

Lou grabbed the paper and followed the map with his finger. "It's an hour away in the other direction. You'd better step it up, Man, or we'll miss our plane."

The cohorts made it to the lake in under 45 minutes. It was more like a swamp, surrounded by high grass, leafless trees, and a few stumps. Green algae floated upon the water; its residue giving off the odor of rotten eggs. Both men gagged as they walked. Their sneakers sank into the soft mud. Mo wondered if he would ever be able to wear them again. He spewed a litany of obscenities until he reached the water's edge with Lou in tow. Mo removed the Glock from the duffle bag and threw it as far out as he was able. It splashed, producing rings of waves and slowly sank to the bottom. The flies scattered in all directions, and the swamp returned to its vegetated state.

The two men reached Sky Harbor and returned the car, before boarding with enough time to clear security. There was no luggage to check in, only one carry on with an empty backpack scrunched inside.

Lou was silent as the two criminals found their seats in coach. Mo mistook the silence for calmness, but his accomplice's countenance told a different story. He remained outraged the entire flight back to Houston, wondering why, when he pulled the trigger, his old friend would take off and leave him laying in the dirt to fend for himself.

~ CHAPTER THIRTY-FOUR ~

The 23rd Precinct was located a few blocks north of Washington Street, in the Downtown area of Phoenix. Detective Sergeant Anthony Paretta had been with his unit for nine years. He was known for his keen sense of discernment and his top-notch background in dealing with felons. However, this case had him baffled. "Who would want to harm a widow and grandmother who had spent the bulk of her life caring for her children and grandchildren?" he asked his colleagues.

Marge's injury was grave but not fatal. She remained in the ICU unit of Valley Hospital on life support. One consolation—the bullet was removed from her lower skull during surgery and sent to the Crime Lab. Detective Anthony Paretta or Tony, the name he preferred, was waiting for identification from ballistics. He had just arrived for the day and began to brief his men as soon as he exited the elevator.

Unlike the old Edwardian architecture of Camwood's 7th Precinct with its small cubicles that kept the desks hidden by the walls that encased them, this building was modern in design with an open floor plan that left little space for privacy. At times, Tony's deep voice could be heard throughout the lower level of the building. "We're waiting for ballistics to get back to us," he informed those on the case. "As soon as we hear from them, we may have a lead. Unfortunately, there were no witnesses. Keep doing what you are doing. Knock on doors. See if anyone heard anything—anything at all. I'm going to pay a visit to her husband's company tomorrow. I'll take one of you with me. They may be able to shed some light on this. Maybe he was the target, not her." He was confident once the bullet could be traced back to the gun from which it was fired, he would have the evidence needed to convict whoever was responsible.

Detective Matt Frasier was one of the men assigned to the Bernside case, and along with Tony, he had been working on it for several days. They had visited Valley Hospital and hoped Marge would be conscious and able to assist them in some way. Hearing she was on life support, they left word for the staff to contact the precinct if she should take a turn for the better.

Matt, who declined any offers to move uptown, had been with Tony for five years and remained on his team. They were fast friends and relied on each other for guidance. Having solved many homicides together, they found the ones with the younger victims were the hardest to deal with. Neither were church goers, but they did believe in a higher power of some sort. Matt's six-foot-four frame over-powered Tony's five-foot-eight-inch stature. Their fellow officers dubbed them Mutt and Jeff, which didn't sit well with either man. Matt was fair haired with grey-green eyes, unmarried, and still single at forty. Tony's Sicilian skin contrasted Matt's. Tony was married fifteen years with two boys. Ryan, his youngest, was twelve; Kyle, the oldest, had turned fourteen that past summer.

"Pull up the file we have on the Bernside case," Tony instructed Matt as he entered his office.

"Sure thing, Sarge." Tony studied Matt's stride as he turned the corner and disappeared from view. "He needs to lose a few pounds," he mumbled. "I'll have to talk to him about all that junk food he keeps on his desk."

Tony's office was located on the second floor. The glass enclosures, void of ceilings, were unable to absorb all the sounds that came out of the room, much to the staff's dismay. Often his voice would disrupt their train of thought, and they were grateful for what little partition separated them from their ability to concentrate, but this day was different. They would be glad to hear the breaking news.

In less than ten minutes, Matt burst through the door of Tony's office with the file in hand, grabbing the attention of his co-workers in the outer area. They jumped to their feet moving closer to the door in time to hear him speak. The shut blinds shielded them from their superiors as they heard Matt's words. "A bulletin just came in downstairs. After questioning several of the neighbors, we hit pay dirt. The family to the left of the Bernsides home had a surveillance system hooked up, and it was able to capture two images running from the side yard the night the Bernside woman was shot. It was dark, but the cameras were equipped with night vision. They were able to pick up two figures heading for the street. That's all I have for now. Maybe with some enhancement the lab might be able to get a positive ID."

"How come I'm the last to find things out around here?" Tony's voice bellowed. "We need to get that tape over to forensics. Let's go."

As the two men bolted out the door, those in ear shot had already scrambled to their desk. They went unnoticed.

Martin Albright and his family had lived next door to the Bernsides for twenty-two years. Although both families did not consider their relationship to be one to write about, they had managed to maintain a mutual respect. Of course, there was the occasional mishaps, like the Albright's Great Dane Bentley, forgetting which lawn was his own, or Marge's feline Daisy, who thought the neighbor's grandchild's sandbox was her territory, but these incidents were rectified swiftly to keep the peace.

Martin's day had begun as usual. A brisk walk to the corner coffee shop to retrieve the morning edition of the Arizona Republic and a quick cup of decaf with the "old cronies," as they were called, and a slower walk back that revealed to him he had better get a complete checkup. Walking through his front door, he handed Evelyn her long-awaited newspaper.

"I was beginning to worry, Martin. You are usually back earlier."

"You know how it is, Ev," he grunted, "another fish story. Only this one was a mile long."

"The fish or the story," she quipped.

"The story of course, and the fish exaggeration even longer." Martin chuckled. Their conversation was interrupted by a loud knock on the door. Having left it open, he had no choice but to greet the two strangers standing under the portico.

"Are you Martin Albright?" the shorter gentleman inquired.

"Why yes, I am."

"Sorry to bother you, Mr. Albright, I'm Detective Anthony Paretta, and this is my partner Detective Frasier. May we come in?"

"Why, of course, please do." Martin guided the two detectives into the living room where Evelyn sat reading her paper. About to cut out an article that caught her attention, she placed the scissors on the coffee table and rose to her feet.

"Evelyn, Dear, this is Detective Paretta, and his partner Detective Frasier.

"I'm happy to know you, Detectives," Evelyn said, extending her hand. "I think I know why you are here. Please sit. Would you gentlemen like something cold to drink or perhaps some coffee?"

Hoping to get right to the point, both men declined the offer. Tony spoke first. "Mrs. Albright, we are here to ask you and your husband if there is anything else you can tell us about the night your neighbor Marge Bernside got shot. Were you were home at the time?"

"I told the officers everything I knew when they stopped by yesterday," Martin interrupted. "At first, my wife and I were not aware of any crime being committed. We both take something to help us sleep before bedtime, and we didn't hear the house alarm go off or the shot. Her alarm has gone off a few times in the past when Marge forgot and opened the door to let the cat out. If I heard the gun go off, I would think it was a car backfiring. We're not used to crime around here." He continued, "We always run through the surveillance tape before deleting anything. That's when we noticed two figures running from her side yard. We immediately called the police and reported it. Two officers stopped by yesterday and said they would follow up. I guess that's where you come in." His worried expression changed to one of deep concern. "Have they found those creeps yet?" he asked, "and how is Marge? Have you heard anything?"

"Not yet," Detective Frasier said. "Can you add anything to what you told the officers yesterday afternoon? What side of the house did you see them running away from?"

"The answer to your question is no. We heard and saw nothing.

We could only hear the TV when we went to bed, which we keep on all night. The tape will show you the direction they were running from. It was the south side of the house.

"Is this true?" Tony turned to Evelyn.

"My husband is right, Detective Paretta. We knew or heard nothing until we saw the tape."

"May I have the tape now?"

"We offered it to the officers yesterday afternoon. They said someone would be by to retrieve it."

Evelyn walked over to the secretary and unlocked the desk. She pulled out a small package from one of the nooks in the desk front and handed it to Tony. He smiled and thanked her. "We'll be in touch." He turned to her husband. "Thank you for your time, Mr. Albright. If you remember anything you think can be helpful please contact us." He handed him his card.

Martin ushered the two detectives to the door and promised to contact them if he and his wife remembered anything that would help in the investigation. Closing the door behind him, he turned to his wife. "Whew!" "Glad that's over with. I do hope that's the end of things."

~ CHAPTER THIRTY-FIVE ~

It was nearly eleven o'clock when he received the call. "This is Forensics, Detective. Better get down here in a hurry." The adrenaline kicked in as Tony dialed Matt's extension.

"Matt, let's go. Forensics hit on something. Meet me at the desk downstairs." By the time Tony reached the front desk, Matt was waiting.

Located on the other end of town, it took the detectives twenty minutes to reach the Forensics Lab. As they entered the building, they were directed to a small room in the basement. Not wanting to wait for the elevator, they bolted through the fire exit and descended the stairs two at a time while the alarm resounded throughout the building. By the time they reached the lower level, the distress signal had been turned off. They approached the north end of the building and followed the arrow directing them to the Image Enhancing Room. A tall grey-haired gentleman approached them. His smile was wide. "You must be Detective Paretta," he said as they entered the room. "And, I see you brought your partner with you. Your arrival was loud and clear." He continued to smile, only this time it was wider.

"Yes, I'm Tony Paretta, and this is my partner Detective Matt Fraiser." His face slightly reddened.

"I'm Eric Austice, and these men are my assistants." He introduced each man respectively. "This is Don, Mike, and Todd. Have a seat. We have something to show you."

Tony and Matt took a seat at a long table under the florescent lighting. They sat facing a white screen. Eric instructed Don to lower the lights and start the tape. The two detectives focused on the images moving about in the darkness. They were surrounded by trees and tall shrubs. "How can you get anything from this?" Matt mocked.

"Were you able to enhance it?" Tony asked.

"Gentlemen, this lab has state of the art equipment. We called you here so you didn't have to wait for the images to be processed, and you can see them first-hand," Eric responded.

As the detectives eyes remained fixed on the screen, the background became lighter and clearer. Don zoomed in on the perpetrators. They witnessed Mo running from the side yard with Lou following close behind. The enhancement was so precise you could see neither man had shaved that day.

Tony banged his fist on the table. "These dudes look familiar." His eyes narrowed. Once they're ID'd I want you to send out an APB to every chief of detectives this side of the borders," he instructed Matt. He shook each man's hand and thanked them for their diligence.

"Gentlemen, will you excuse us? We have some homework to do. Send us a copy pronto, so we can get started." He turned toward his partner. "Let's go, we have to hit the books. I've seen these guys somewhere before."

It took several days for ballistics to get back to the detective. During that time Tony was able to place names on the faces shown to him by the Forensic Lab. As he sat in his glass enclosed world, feet elevated, cigarette dangling out of the left side of his mouth, he dialed Matt's extension. "Hey, Buddy, get up here STAT. I have some good news."

In less than a minute, Matt came barreling through the door. Tony was passionate as he spoke. "It didn't take long for the system to cough up these two jokers," Tony said. Matt remained silent as his superior filled him in on the details. "Does the name Digbey mean anything to you?" he asked.

Matt thought for a while. "Digbey—Digbey," he repeated, "Yeah, sounds familiar. Wasn't he the guy that did 25 in state prison for being an accessory?"

"That's him. He went by another name though. Do you remember it?"

"It's on the tip of my tongue—take me out of my misery."

"It was Mo, Frank 'Mo' Digbey. He aided and abetted a homicide," Tony added. "His buddy did the dirty work, and Mo did the driving."

"Who's the other guy?"

"His name is Lou Parisi, aka Louie Paris. I guess he didn't like the accommodations in the free world—he's going back."

Tony continued, "When I went home last night, I couldn't sleep. I kept thinking. Where did I know these guys from? Then I remembered. Well over 20 years ago, I was working another unit, and a case had me baffled. Some guns were stolen from a warehouse in downtown Phoenix. We found out later they were shipped out to Texas. They were sold in the Panhandle for triple the price. Lou Parisi was involved. He ended up getting extra time for drug trafficking and gun smuggling after they indicted him on murder. He had just popped a dealer. Someone snitched."

"Then how did Mo Digbey fit into this?" Matt asked.

"I heard at one point the two were cellmates. They were sent to different facilities, and each thought the other was still doing time. Lou was released months ago. He must have gotten wind Mo was out and contacted him. Most likely he was desperate. He's been shacking up at his great aunt's house. Couldn't handle it, I guess. That's when they hooked up. They both had connections in Texas. Houston PD is on it as we speak. There's another person of interest they are looking at— Thomas Black, aka Tex Black, a real cowboy. They both had dealings with him a few years ago. He did a couple of short stints for credit card fraud and bad checks. As soon as I hear from Houston, I'll fill you in."

Matt smiled. "Looks like this will be wrapped up in no time." He turned to leave.

"Most likely," Tony replied.

~ CHAPTER THIRTY-SIX ~

The alarm on the IV pump startled Marge out of her sleep. Still unsure of her surroundings, she opened her swollen eyes and peered around the room. A short, dark-haired nurse, approached her bed and smiled. "Good morning, Mrs. Burnside. Did you have a good sleep?"

"Where am I?" Marge was terrified.

"You're at Valley Hospital, Mrs. Bernside. Do you remember? I'm your nurse, Terry. I'll be on duty until tonight. If you need anything, press this button." She placed the call button in Marge's hands. After she was sure Marge understood, she pinned it to the side of the sheet and carried on with her duties.

Marge eyed Terry as she checked the IV pump, changed the bag, straightened the covers, and wrote something down in the chart hanging at the foot of the bed. She was in pain. Her confusion made her unable to unscramble any thoughts she had. Her mind was a blank slate." Terry, do you know why I'm here?" she asked, tearfully.

Terry smiled. "Dr. Alonso will be in to discuss that with you this morning. He's your attending physician. If you need to talk to him right now, I can have him paged."

The staff had been advised by Harry, Jr. not to speak of the circumstances that brought Marge to the Hospital until she was ready to comprehend what had happened to her. Until law enforcement solved the case, there was not that much to tell. Marge was shot in the head. By whom Harry, Jr. didn't know, and for what reason he didn't know either. What he did know was his mother had been through hell and recently taken off life support. He wanted to be sure she was strong enough to grasp what took place. It could wait.

Marge had been found by the EMT's on the den floor. Harry, Jr. had insisted on her wearing a medical alert button around her neck, and she wore it faithfully. After the bullet hit her lower right skull, she fell to the floor. At the exact moment of impact, she grabbed the pendant and it reacted. Whether she was cognizant at that time and willfully pressed the alarm or whether it was a kind of miracle remains to be seen. The fact is it alerted the medics. Within ten minutes the emergency team broke through her front door. By the time they reached the den, she had already lost consciousness. It was obvious she had a head wound. The EMT's attended to Marge as she was transported to the hospital. They applied pressure to the gaping hole in her right skull area and administered oxygen and fluids on the way to the ER. She was still breathing. They left it up to the doctors to decide what might have happened to her.

After receiving calls from several neighbors of a gunshot being fired, the authorities showed up at the same time as the EMT's. One officer did an extensive search outside the house and found a shell casing lying in the side yard near the broken den window. By that time Marge had been admitted to Valley Hospital and intubated. She was placed on a ventilator and prepped for surgery.

The nursing assistant completed Marge's bath and turned her on her side. She applied lotion gently onto her back. She repositioned her and emptied the drainage bag on the side of the bed. After straightening the covers, she excused herself. Marge managed a weak smile. "I would like to rest now," she whispered.

Terry, who had just entered the room, heard the request. "You do that," she said. "Dr. Alonso will be in to see you when he makes his rounds." She walked over to Marge and patted her hand. She smiled and disappeared. Marge was left to struggle with her thoughts, trying to fit the pieces together.

It was 11:30 a.m. when Dr. Alonso walked into Marge's room. A covered lunch tray remained untouched on her bedside table. "Not hungry?" he asked. "I thought after several days your appetite would return."

"I'm not hungry, Doctor."

"You'll never get it back if you don't start somewhere. Please try and eat something. I'll arrange for a volunteer to come and help."

Marge ignored the offer. "Doctor, will you please tell me what I'm doing here?"

Adhering to Harry, Jr.'s wishes, the doctor remained evasive. "Your son will be in to see you this afternoon."

After examining Marge, Dr. Alonso took her hands in his. He tried to reassure her. "Now, you get some rest." He walked over to the sink and began to wash his hands. He took a paper towel from the dispenser and peered over his shoulder. He observed Marge trying to touch the back of her head, hindered by the large bandages that encompassed it. She had no idea of the gravity of her wound. She hadn't been told she was shot and had not looked into a mirror. She awkwardly began to pull on the strands of gauze which were intertwined in a tight zig-zag pattern, secured with tape. "Oh my," she cried out. "Doctor, what happened to me?"

At that moment, Harry, Jr. walked into the room and straight to his mother's bedside. Dr. Alonso was relieved and excused himself, leaving Mother and Son to sort it out. Harry Jr. had been designated to be Health Care Proxy for Marge and responsible for all her healthcare decisions. He was grateful that Dr. Alonso was abiding by his wishes.

Marge began to weep, flailing her arms and trying to grab her son's neck. "Harry, why am I here? What happened?"

Harry, Jr. remained silent for a moment. He walked to the window and gazed down four levels to the street below. The day was overcast. He lingered for about a minute and adjusted the blinds. Dragging an empty chair to the bedside, he sat. His words were delicate but confusing to Marge. "Mother, we haven't gotten all the details yet. You've had an accident. You have a head wound, and the doctors have been taking care of it. When you are stronger, we can talk about it." Leaning over the bed, he gave his mother a hug. He promised to visit her again that evening. "The children send their love. We'll try and get them up to see you soon."

Harry, Jr. had been traveling when he received the phone call. Being a buyer for a large department store chain, his travels took him to many different parts of the U.S. and Europe. His company covered all the expenses, but his boss had the habit of booking him on red eye flights. When he was informed of his mother's accident, he was in Germany at a small hotel in Landsthul. The quaint town was situated 6 miles west of Kaiserslautern. He was scheduled to attend a trade show in Frankfurt that week in hopes he would hook up with some vendors and exporters who would be willing to make a deal. In order to save a dollar, his company sent him to the small German town. Being an Army Vet., Harry didn't mind. Landsthul, and nearby Kaiserslautern, catered to the American Military who had helped to boost the economy in the smaller towns. He also liked the fact that the Landstuhl Regional Medical Center, an Army run hospital, was nearby. He knew they cared for many of the soldiers that came in from Iraq and Afghanistan. He was staying five miles from Ramstein Air Force Base and enjoyed visiting it when he was in town. Even though the higher-ups thought they were being frugal, Harry, Jr. was having a good time.

As soon as he received the call, he bought his own ticket back to Phoenix. He wasn't about to wait for the company to book him on another red eye. Trying to comprehend why this tragedy could have occurred, he was devastated and racking his brain. He hired a car to drive the hour and twenty minutes to the airport. During that time he couldn't cry—not one tear. He was still in shock. It lasted the entire eight hour flight home.

Harry, Jr. had arranged for a taxi to meet him at Sky Harbor Airport and take him directly to the hospital. He was unable to see Marge. She had been brought to the ICU Unit as soon as she was wheeled out of the recovery room, and she was being monitored closely. The bullet had been removed, and he was assured by her surgeon she was expected to recover from her wound. When he arrived, she was still under the effects of the anesthesia. He was told to go home, get some sleep, and return the following day.

The afternoon had turned cooler. The Arizona leaves began to take on their yellow and golden hues, with splashes of red and orange here and there. Harry Jr. rode the hospital elevator down to the main floor. He chose not to go directly home. He drove toward the Phoenix Police Department to speak to Detective Anthony Paretta, who had made the call to Landstuhl. He wanted answers. Who would target an older widow? What could they possibly want? Was the bullet meant for his father instead? What was it law enforcement was not telling him? Why didn't he take Sergeant Paretta's phone call serious? No matter what the answers were, he was determined to find out who the criminal was who pulled the trigger.

~ CHAPTER THIRTY-SEVEN ~

Sergeant Larry O'Donnell ended the call and sank back in his chair. *Thank God, this week is almost over.* He was looking forward to a good game on TV, a few beers, and some down time. He continued to prioritize the stack of files on his desk only to be interrupted by another call.

"Camwood Police, Sergeant O'Donnell." He was annoyed he had picked up the receiver.

"Sergeant, this is the Pheonix 23rd Precinct calling, Detective Sergeant Anthony Paretta. You had contacted us awhile ago and asked us to look into the safety of a widow here in Phoenix." He paused. "We found no reason to have her put under surveillance. We notified her son to keep an eye out and let us know of any suspicions he may have. He had an alarm system installed after the death of his father and felt confident that there was no reason why she would be in danger of any kind. She had no enemies. Other than hearsay, we had no evidence."

"I understand. Thank you for the update."

"Wait a minute, I'm not finished. Things have since changed. There's been an attempted murder on her life. At first, we thought the perpetrators were after her dead husband, but after careful consideration it seems they were targeting her. They were under the impression she witnessed an exchange of drugs and wanted to silence her. They were caught on tape. We put out an APB on them, and they were apprehended in Houston last night—one at the home of his great aunt and the other at some flea bag above a pool hall. One of these jokers, a Louis Parisi, aka, Louie Paris, started to talk."

"I think I know what comes next."

"I'm almost there. It seems a Thomas Black, aka, Tex Black, hired an ex-con named Frank Digbey, otherwise known as Mo, to pop the Bernside woman here in Phoenix. Digbey got Parisi involved. After drilling him, he caved and led the detectives on the case to Black. They found him in a dive outside of Houston. He started talking and pointed the finger in your direction."

Larry took off his jacket and pulled his chair closer to his desk. "I'm all ears," he said. "Go ahead, Detective. Hit me."

"All these guys did time together, and they managed to keep in touch. This guy Tex was hired by one of your own to target the Bernside woman."

"I can take it."

"He's claiming a Joe Balboa hired him to do her in."

Larry took a few seconds for it to register. Chen was telling me the truth. Then he spoke. "Fax me all the information you have, Detective. We've been doing an internal investigation of our department, and he's been a person of interest." His thoughts raced like a clueless child about to answer the last question in a spelling bee. His last words to Detective Tony Paretta were, "Keep me posted."

This was the break Larry had been waiting for. He sat stoically for at least ten minutes. "I knew it," he said aloud. He tilted his head back—his smile was wide. He hadn't smiled like that in a year. "I said I'd get you Balboa," he mumbled. Detective Paretta had informed him all three men had court appointed attorneys. So now it was a matter of waiting. Once again, Larry picked up the phone, but this time it was he who was making the call.

"Robbie, it's me. Get downtown now. Make it fast."

"Are you kidding, Sarge? I'm off to the lake with the family. You know how it is," he said.

"Trust me. You'll want to hear this. The lake will still be there tomorrow. What I have to tell you will make your vacation even better."

~ 170 ~

~ CHAPTER THIRTY-EIGHT ~

Sarah was delayed in traffic for over an hour. By the time she pulled into the driveway, she was exhausted and famished. She approached the living room and noticed Niki had dozed off on the couch. "I spoke to her two minutes ago. I'd give anything to fall asleep that fast." Not wanting to disturb her, she tiptoed to the kitchen and started to prepare dinner.

Sarah had been working in the import/export business for twenty-one years and was respected by her co-workers and supervisors. Her expertise included finding lost shipments on the northern piers of a nearby port of entry and arranging their clearance through U.S. Customs. She was a troubleshooter. She loved her work and she occasionally used her free time to visit the docks and converse with the longshoremen, sometimes sharing a sandwich and coffee with them while she watched the ocean liners and freighters glide by.

In her younger days, she would daydream of being on one of these great ships and sailing off to faraway places. As her responsibilities mounted in raising a young daughter alone, she put her fantasies on hold. She considered each day an adventure. Growing closer to her God equipped her in facing the problems that came her way. Looking to her Savior, who was always on duty, helped her to face them head on.

The phone rang. Sarah was removing the casserole from the oven.
Hearing it, Niki yelled for her mother to get it.

"It's Chen, Niki. Do you want to take it?"

"I overslept, tell him I'll meet him at Chasins at eight."

"What about dinner?"

"I forgot about our date tonight. Would you mind if we have the
casserole tomorrow night? I'd better get ready." She dashed upstairs.

"Not at all, I'll grab something quick." She placed the hot dish into
fridge, ignoring the old wives' tale about having to cool things off first.
Scanning the local paper and finding nothing of interest, she opened
a can of tomato soup and a package of saltine crackers. A ring at the
door interrupted thoughts. Gazing through the magnifier, she saw Chen
standing on the front porch.

Sarah was praying about the relationship her daughter had with the
junior detective. Niki had not told her about Chen's tainted past, and she
was unaware of his conversion. Opening the door, she welcomed him
and invited him into the living room. She called out to Niki that Chen
had arrived.

"Tell him I'm not ready, Mom," she yelled back. "I was supposed to
meet him at Chasins. Can you keep him busy?"

"How have you been, Chen," Sarah asked.

"I'm fine, Mrs. Hughes. I had a change in plans tonight and
decided to pick Niki up here. I'm glad I caught you home. I wanted
to talk to you privately."

Sarah was clueless—she remained cordial. "Of course, would you
like to go outside in the garden?"

"That won't be necessary. Do you mind if I sit here," he pointed to
the love seat.

"Please do."

Chen's hands were damp. He tried tucking them into the cushions of
the sofa and hoped she wouldn't notice. "Mrs. Hughes, Niki and I haven't
known each other very long, but I have grown to love her very much.
Because her father is not here, I have come to ask your permission. I want
to ask her to marry me, and I would like your blessing."

"Have you told her how you feel," Sarah asked.

"Not yet. I wanted to speak to you first. I plan on telling her tonight."

Sarah felt from the beginning of their relationship Chen's feelings were far deeper than her daughter's. Could she be wrong? In recent weeks, Niki hadn't mentioned him much, and she had no way of knowing where they stood. "Chen, I know you care for Niki, and I've noticed she smiles often and seems content. This is a decision you both have to agree on. If you have sought the Lord and have a peace about it, follow your heart."

Chen tried to conceal his surprise. Sarah caught the look. He did not expect her blessing—not this soon. He walked over to her and gave her a tight hug. "Mrs. Hughes, I can't tell you how happy you've made me."

"Now you run along and have a good time. I will stay here and pray you are both in God's will."

"What are you two talking about?" Niki interrupted, as she bolted into the room. "Sorry, I'm late."

"Just small talk," Chen answered. "I've had a change in plans. Let's get going before it gets too late."

"Where are we going?"

"You will see," Chen winked at her mother. "It's a surprise." He smiled, exposing his pure white teeth.

Niki chuckled. "I love surprises."

Sarah looked on as the young couple descended the porch steps and strolled to Chen's car. She watched them drive away; she began to pray. "Father, if this is Your will, make it clear to them. If not, close the door."

Sarah was looking forward to some alone time. She spent the rest of the evening cutting out coupons and scanning through some articles. Her Bible remained on the kitchen table, and she decided to read some Scriptures before retiring. She opened to the book of Romans. She read aloud, "How then shall they call on Him in whom they have not believed? And how shall they believe in Him of whom they have not heard? And how shall they hear without a preacher?" Sarah thought of Chen. She knew Niki's objective was to bring the Word of God to him and prayed God's will be done in both their lives. She realized early in her spiritual walk it is better to go straight to the Source than to dance around any issues she may have and try and fix them herself. Her desire for Niki was she would not be unequally yoked. Sometimes she is faithful in following her formula, other times not, but her goal in life is to try to overcome the nots "Go to the Source when you have a problem," she taught her daughter. "He hears every prayer. Sometime He may say yes, sometime He may say no, and sometime He may say be patient, you haven't learned what I want to teach you yet. His decisions are always best for our lives." She would end her mini sermon with the following: "He sees the big picture. We don't. You know, it's like playing a board game, follow the directions, go to the source. Don't stop along the way."

A breeze swept across Niki's face. She lowered the window of the tan sedan. "This is miles away from Chasins" she remarked.

Chen continued to look straight ahead, trying not to smile. "I wanted to finish what I started to tell you on the phone about the case, and I didn't want to discuss it anywhere we may run into familiar faces."

"I agree," Niki replied, still a bit puzzled.

Chen pulled into the narrow driveway that led to the rear of La Bella's, a favorite spot his parents used to frequent. It was a seaside eatery, specializing in Italian Cuisine. City folk were known to drive two hours to enjoy the succulent seafood menu, which included fresh caught crab legs, mussels, and calamari dipped and fried to perfection in a light batter. They would listen to soft music, sip wine, and watch the fishermen coast into the harbor from the outside balcony as the sun set. Though there were many eating spots on the pier, when referred to as the "restaurant on the water," everyone knew it meant La Bella's. Chen decided it was here he would ask Niki to spend the rest of her life with him.

After the couple enjoyed a superb dinner of stuffed salmon and Florentine asparagus, Chen began to describe in detail everything Sergeant Larry O'Donnell had told him. When I think you could have been shot…" His voice was brittle. Avoiding her eyes, he gazed out the window at the small boats docked on the pier.

"So I was a target also?" Niki interrupted. "I was afraid Mom and I would be in danger."

Chen grabbed Niki's hand and held it tight. He revealed how Marge Bernside was targeted, and that the men responsible for shooting her were being held in custody in a Houston jail.

"Oh, that poor woman," Niki was on the verge of tears. "Will she make it?"

"I'm not sure. I don't have all the details yet."

"Chen, we have to pray for her. I hope this wasn't the surprise you were talking about."

"No, of course not. It's something else—good news I hope."

"You didn't have to drag me halfway across the country to tell me. Chasins would have been close enough."

"No, it wouldn't have." Chen said. "I wanted the atmosphere to be right."

"What are you talking about?"

"First of all, did I tell you how beautiful you look tonight?"

"Once in the car, but if you want to say it again, go ahead. I love hearing it."

"You do look exceptionally beautiful tonight. By the way, I have something for you. I picked it out myself." A soft Italian instrumental played, and the sound of mandolins made the occasion even more memorable. Niki's face flushed, and she held her breath. She looked on as he reached into the side pocket of his jacket and pulled out a small white box. He handed it across the table to the lady he hoped would be his future bride. Her hands vibrated as she opened the lid, exposing a white pear-shaped diamond, flanked by baguettes. Chen wasted no time. "Niki, will you marry me?" he asked. His voice shook—his expression priceless.

There was no hesitation in Niki's voice. "Yes, yes, I will."

As they drove home, neither spoke. A feeling of peace and contentment overwhelmed them. Niki's thoughts turned to her mother. Sensing her deep thought, Chen spoke, "What's troubling you, Niki? Is it your mother?"

"What makes you say that?"

"You can't fool me. Something's wrong."

"Yes, what if she doesn't approve? I mean, after all, we haven't known each other that long."

"Niki, your mom and I had a talk before we left tonight. She told me she would pray for the Lord's will in our lives and she wanted you to be happy. He gripped her hand. Are you happy?"

"Blissfully."

Chen held onto Niki's hand the remainder of the ride home. As she leaned her head back, she closed her eyes and entered into her prayer closet. *Lord, please help me to keep the peace I am feeling right now. Have it remain with me, free of obstacles. I pray our marriage will be blessed by You and by our loved ones.* A tear managed to find its way to the corner of her eye and trickle down her cheek. Wiping it away, she smiled.

Chen pulled up to the Hughes residence and turned off the motor of the two-door sedan. Turning to Niki, he leaned over and kissed her. "Call me tomorrow and let me know how things go."

All the lights were off, except for a small light near the stairs that lead to the second floor. Niki passed her mother's bedroom and stopped. Hearing nothing, she continued on to her room. Closing the door behind her, she threw herself on the bed. She turned over and stared at the ceiling for a good while. "How blessed I am," she whispered.

The sun ducked behind the clouds and out again, the ritual continuing throughout the morning. Unable to contain her emotions, Niki showered, dressed, and hurried downstairs to the kitchen. The smell of fresh brewed coffee filled the empty room. She walked over to the window and glanced out. She spotted Sarah on her knees digging in the back garden. Bolting through the door she ran to her. "Mom, get up. Come inside, please," she shouted.

Sarah had spent the last two hours loosening the hard-brown earth and lining up the rows for her fall planting. Niki extended her hand and gently pulled her mother up. She coaxed her to come inside. The clouds had exhausted themselves, and the sun became brighter as it rose in the heavens. Maybe it was its reflection that blinded Sarah and caused her to miss the sparkling gem on Niki's right hand but missed it she did.

"What's this all about, Nik?"

"Mom, remember when you said you wanted me to be happy no matter what?"

"Yes, I do."

"I have watched Chen grow over the past few weeks, and he has not only grown as a responsible human being, he has grown in Christ. After we had dinner, we took a ride by a lake where some of his college buddies used to fish. It wasn't far from the restaurant we ate at. It was there he confided to me he wants to go into the ministry. He is so grateful to the Lord, he wants to devote the rest of his life to winning souls for God's Kingdom. He wants to attend Bible college during the evenings and take the day shift at work. Eventually he wants to go into full-time ministry. I can't even imagine being a minister's wife."

Sarah smiled and hugged her daughter. "A minister's wife is a hard life. If God calls you to that vocation, He will give you the grace to withstand the pressures. Aren't you thinking a little far ahead?"

Niki held up her hand to expose the pear-shaped diamond for her mother to see. Tearfully they embraced, and the twinkle in Niki's eyes far surpassed the beam in Sarah's smile.

~ CHAPTER THIRTY-NINE ~

Sergeant Larry O'Donnell sat back in his chair with his eyes fixated on the slow drip coming from a corner of the ceiling. He stood and placed a used coffee cup under it and phoned maintenance. It had rained non-stop for two days, and the office was cold and damp. Larry opened his desk drawer and pulled out his inhaler. He had never been diagnosed with asthma. He was given the medication and instructed to use it when his wheezing flared up. This day was no exception. Giving the canister a few shakes, he exhaled deeply and sucked in the medicine. The treatment seemed to work. His breathing improved, and he left himself a memo to renew the prescription.

Larry had not heard from Chen since the day he decided to look the other way. He had placed him on desk duty uptown and was anxious to put him back in circulation. Chen knew he was being observed and was intent on proving to Larry he could be trusted. The sergeant had few he could trust. Giving the young detective a break was not easy for him, but he chose to go with his gut feeling. He never questioned what Chen did with the money he made off Joe Balboa. He believed his conversion was real, and he knew he would make up the spent money in his own way.

"Detective Young," Larry barked.

"Yes, Sir?"

"O'Donnell here. Are you ready to go back to active duty?"

Chen smiled. "You bet, Sir. Ready as I'll ever be."

"Get down here, and we can get started."

That day was a turning point for Chen. All the fears and insecurities he was harboring left him. Trusting the Lord had honored his repentance, he reaffirmed his promise to serve Him faithfully.

Chen was so wrapped up in his thoughts of seeing Niki on this night that he passed the intersection of 12th and Main. The massive courthouse with its huge white columns and marble steps leading to the front entrance reminded him he had gone too far. He knew he was late. He raced up to Larry's office and found him dozing in his leather swivel chair. For a moment he thought he was in a deep sleep, until he noticed the sergeant's blue orbs still visible between his lids.

Hearing Chen come in, Larry sat upright. "Pull up a chair," he instructed the detective.

Chen pulled over one of the metal chairs that stood against the wall. He remained quiet, almost pious as he awaited the news he was so urgently summoned downtown for.

Larry leaned forward. His eyes wildly revealed he had information that could help determine the outcome of the investigation into drug trafficking within the department.

"Detective Young," Larry's brow furrowed, and his eyes peered straight into Chen's, "the gamut has run full circle." Looking puzzled, Chen remained silent. "A few hours ago, I received a phone call from Detective Sergeant Anthony Paretta of the Phoenix Police Department. He's working together with the Houston Department and a Sergeant Paul Conway. He has a suspect in custody. It's the cowboy, Tex Black. He may be the connection to who masterminded the murder attempt on the Bernside woman." Larry filled him in on all the details that Detective Paretta gave him. "I'm canceling my plans for the weekend and staying put. I have a few calls to make. If Houston cuts a deal with the suspect and he makes a positive ID of Joe Balboa, we are halfway home. They are checking his phone and computer records as I speak, hoping to tie him to Balboa. They had to cross paths at some time." Now we play the waiting game."

Larry knew if Tex Black didn't cooperate, he would have to use his original plan and send Chen undercover. "If he doesn't play along, I'll have to ask you to keep your part of the bargain."

"Sarge, what if Balboa identifies me as an accomplice?"

"I've thought about that myself," Larry looked as concerned as Chen. "I have it covered. I'll tell them you were working for me." Seeing the expression on Chen's face, he added, "The lie will be mine. Don't worry. Anyway, it's no longer a lie. It was your last planned assignment. Remember?"

The two men shook hands and parted. Chen knew if Tex pointed to Joe Balboa, and it stuck, he could move on with his life a free spirit.

~ CHAPTER FORTY ~

Houston headquarters was located two hundred yards from a major highway in the downtown area. Sergeant Paul Conway had worked side by side with the homicide division for ten years. Taking a different approach than Anthony Paretta of Phoenix, and Camwood's Larry O'Donnell, he would attempt to handle the bulk of the tough cases himself. At first, he would delve into them like a tenacious bull heading straight for its target and calling for assistance when he had exhausted all possibilities of solving a case on his own. His fellow officers ended up in the field, almost daily, asking the hard questions.

The temperature had risen to 90 degrees. Scanning through the pile of files he had accumulated, Sergeant Conway sat at his desk. They were all unsolved cases. He reached into his front pocket, pulled out a hanky, and pressed it to his brow. Picking up the phone, he dialed the extension that would connect him to maintenance. "How long does it take for you guys to check out the a/c? It hasn't worked all morning." His eyes narrowed and his lips tightened. "If you guys don't get to it now, you'll pay in blood for it—you hear?"

"We're working on it," was the response.

Sergeant Conway banged the receiver down and walked over to the window. He retrieved a water bottle out of the mini fridge under the sill and guzzled half of the pristine liquid. He felt the dryness in his throat dissipate. Gazing out the window, he viewed the city he loved and worked so hard to protect. *Think I'll call it a day if these incompetent clowns don't fix this system.* Interrupted by the phone ringing, he picked up the receiver. "Conway here...who? Yeah, what can I do for you, Sergeant?"

"This is Sergeant Anthony Paretta from Phoenix Headquarters," Tony repeated. "I wanted to touch base with you again. How's the investigation going with your suspects? Anything new?"

"Nothing new since we spoke. We're holding Mo Digbey and Lou Parisi in custody along with Tex Black. The state has appointed lawyers to represent them, and you know where that leaves us. Most likely they will cop a plea." Sergeant Conway walked over to a small mirror on his desk, picked up a broken comb and began to stroke his thick salt and pepper moustache. "Digbey wouldn't talk at first, now he is pointing the finger at Black and accusing him of being the mastermind of the plot to kill the Bernside woman. Black sang an aria about the perp in Camwood's Precinct—what's his name—Balboa? I thought we gave you all that information."

"Yes, we have all that. I spoke to O'Donnell in Camwood, ten minutes ago. He's just as anxious to nail this guy so he'll never ride in a patrol car again, much less walk the beat." He stopped for a moment. "The reason I called is we are hoping to get Tex Black to make a positive identification of Joe Balboa . Sergeant O'Donnell faxed over some pictures for you to look at and requested you pass them on to the attorneys handling their case. I'm sending photos of the victim before and after the shooting."

"We'll do our best—we'll get back to both of you." Sergeant Conway responded. He hung up and sat quietly for several minutes. He stared at the images of his two daughters on the bookcase across from his desk. Melody was about to turn thirteen, and sixteen-year-old Krissy had applied for her driver's license. He had promised to take the girls to a concert at the Grand Arena on the weekend, and the thought of being stuck in the office for any reason haunted him. He walked into the outer office and went directly to the fax machine. Several pictures of Joe Balboa lay in the receiving tray, in and out of uniform. He was thankful.

It was known to the authorities Tex Black didn't have a permanent address. He had moved around from motel to motel. He always paid for his stays in cash. They were aware, for the most part, there would be no paper trail. He didn't have a job history to speak of or a family to contact, and the only alias he had used was Tex. Besides gambling and drug dealing, he had made his living preying on widowed women. In order to speed things up, Sergeant Conway called in two detectives. It took them several days to locate the drifter. He was tracked down through a Houston pawn shop owner one of the detectives had decided to question. Tex was brought in on a Friday afternoon on charges of violating his parole with the charge of attempted murder pending. He was grilled for several hours in a small cubicle at the beginning of a hallway on the main floor of the building—and he broke. His song was music to Sergeant Paul Conway's ears. He was given the alternative of a long incarceration if he didn't cooperate. "Listen, you don't have to go away for a long time," he was told. "We can cut a deal." The sergeant motioned to one of the detectives to start the tape recorder.

Through the interrogation of one of the other two suspects, the Houston detectives were told the Glock had been thrown in a man-made lake, located about an hour outside of Phoenix. They had picked it up at a shop somewhere near the airport. It could have been revenge on Lou Parisi's part, for Mo leaving him in the dirt in front of the Bernside home. The reason unknown, but squeal he did. Sergeant Tony Paretta was informed. He sent his team to retrieve the weapon. It was sent to forensics for analysis.

Detectives Geraldine Walsh and Timothy Ironsides had been assigned to the case to canvass the local pawn shops close to Sky Harbor Airport. Arriving late in the afternoon, the two detectives scouted for a parking space and began their search.

The sky darkened, as they approached the sixth and final shop on Tony Paretta's list. "This is right out of a Bogart movie," Timothy glanced at his partner. Geraldine was still looking upward; her eyes were fixated on the old pawn shop sign that hung lopsided over the glass door.

"Anyone could break into this place in a heartbeat and steal all the guns they wanted, Geraldine muttered. Timothy agreed. As they walked into the worn-out shop, the bells overhead rang out, startling the proprietor who had dozed off after a day of no sales—not even a phone call.

Theodore Feldman had been in the pawn business for over forty years. He took great pains to categorize every sale, especially when it came to firearms. Besides the usual names and addresses of buyers and the type of gun he was selling them, he would take a photo of each weapon as he packaged it in the back room, unbeknownst to the buyer waiting out front. That rule was for strangers, of course. If he happened to know you, things were different.

As the two detectives walked into the store, Feldman jumped to his feet. He hoped the encounter would end in a profitable sale. "Good afternoon, how can I be of service to you both?" He forgot to smile.

"We're here to investigate an attempted murder which took place in Phoenix. My name is Timothy Ironsides, and this is my partner Detective Geraldine Walsh. We would like to ask you a few questions."

"Theodore Feldman here," he extended his hand.

"Have you seen this man?" Timothy handed him a 4x6 photo of Mo Digbey, "or this one," showing a larger image of Lou Parisi.

He stared at the photos for a few seconds and shook his head from side to side. He took two steps back. His eyelids fluttered as he spoke. "Ask on. I have nothing to hide."

"Mr. Feldman, we are not accusing you of anything. We are merely asking if you have seen these two men." It was then that the detectives sensed he was lying.

"May we have a look at your books?" Geraldine asked.

Feldman's hands trembled. He pulled a large black book from the wooden shelf behind the counter. "These are my latest entries," he said. "See for yourself," handing the book to Geraldine.

"May I sit over there?" She pointed to a small table near the back room.

"Be my guest."

Both detectives scanned each page but found nothing. They still weren't convinced. Feldman eyed them like a hawk and removed the scowl from his face only to answer the phone, return, and grimace again.

"Thank you for your time, Mr. Feldman."

"We may be back to speak to you again if we need to," Geraldine added.

As they walked toward the car, Timothy spoke first. "Did you see those books, Geri?" Every detail was meticulously written, yet nothing on the Glock."

"That's because he didn't document it," Geraldine said. "He was lying."

Timothy looked at her and nodded. "I bet with a little digging, the sarge can link this hell hole all the way down the I-10 to Tex Black and his two clowns, and close it up for good."

~ CHAPTER FORTY-ONE ~

Detective Robbie Banks bolted into Sergeant Larry O'Donnell's office with a Styrofoam cup in hand. "Enjoy your weekend, Sarge?" he asked. "Here's your cup of joe, black, no sugar."

Larry took the cup, gratefully. "What about you?" he asked.

"Had mine already."

"Let's get cracking. The day's getting shorter by the minute." Larry pressed hard on the intercom. "Cathy, bring the usual."

Cathy Fringe had been his secretary since Larry became head of his department. She was forty-eight and single. She was efficient in running the office; however, she had a reputation of messing up the filing department, which caused chaos and was evident from the long list of missing files. Cathy was also known for her personality. She was a bit nerdy, whimsical, and well liked. Her wardrobe consisted of mid-century clothing in a slew of colors and styles. Even her eyeglasses were right out of a 1950's catalogue. It was no wonder she inherited the nickname "Cat Eyes."

The moment Larry released the intercom, Cathy appeared in the doorway with a huge glass of orange juice. Looking puzzled, Robbie eyed the cup of coffee on the desk.

"Don't worry Banks, it won't go to waste. I haven't had my fix yet."

"I didn't know you've taken to oj, Sarge."

Sergeant O'Donnell sat back in his chair with both arms behind his head. He placed his feet onto the desk on top of several files. He turned his head from side to side and winced. "I have to get to the chiropractor this week. The kink in my neck is back."

Cathy tapped her foot. He caught her impatient glance. "Thanks, Cathy." He pointed to the one small space available on his desk. "Leave it there."

"Careful, Sarge, don't knock it over with your big foot. By the way, this came for you this morning." She handed him the small brown package she had been holding in her other hand. Thinking her comment about his foot was funny, she chuckled and threw the package on the desk. She barely missed the coffee cup.

"And, my feet are not big," Larry yelled as Cathy exited the room.

"Expecting a gift?" Robbie asked.

"Not that I know of," Larry said. "Hmmm—let me see—maybe it's a bomb."

"If it is, you could dismantle it with a bobby pin—it's that small."

Larry carefully picked up the box and placed it to his ear.

"I wouldn't do that if I were you."

"Get out of here Robbie. I don't need you around this morning."

"Not on your life, I'm not leaving until you open that thing."

"Step away then, or you might get your head blown off."

The package was unmarked. It had been hand delivered by a courier, according to Cathy. Larry was confident there was nothing to be concerned about. He placed the package down and slowly pulled on the strings holding the brown paper intact." Hand me the scissors," he ordered Robbie, pointing to the bookcase next to the water cooler. His colleague watched as the Detective cut the last two strings. The paper stripped itself from its package, revealing a small flat box. Larry was gentle as he lifted the top and found it contained a tape with a white sticker attached. The print on the label read: "Interrogation tape of Thomas "Tex" Black." The sergeant could feel his blood pressure rise. "You'd better pull up a chair. You're going to want to stay for this."

The two men sat spellbound as they listened to the Texan's confession. Less than half-way through the tape, they gasped when they heard the words: "Who hired you. Mr. Black? Who hired you as a hit man?" The voice was that of Sergeant Paul Conway.

The answer came back loud and clear. "It was Joe Balboa, one of Camwood's own," Tex's tone was scornful.

"Is this the man you are accusing?" Sargeant Conway had asked, showing Tex the pictures he received from Larry O'Donnell.

"That's him!"

"Houston wasted no time," Larry said. He shut the recorder.

The department's outer office was abuzz with talk. The entire staff had showed up on time for a change, and their chatter could be heard throughout the room. Keyboards pounded at each desk with the noises of fax machines spewing their messages, some important, some not, which added to the turbulence. Amid all the distractions each person sensed something big was going on in the inner room. The two detectives had been in there longer than usual. The staff surmised that big news was about to break.

No exchange of words occurred as the tape played out. Larry never took his eyes off Robbie and studied his demeanor until it ended. "Call Phoenix for me and thank Sergeant Paretta for sending me a copy of the tape," he instructed his colleague. His troubled expression turned to one of triumph. "We got him—we finally got the snake!" he roared.

"Bravo, Sarge," then quoting the Good Book, Robbie raised his eyebrows and uttered, "...be sure your sin will find you out."

~ CHAPTER FORTY-TWO ~

The northeastern sky was devoid of clouds when the alarm in Niki's room rang. Usually she would lie in bed for a half an hour or longer but not on this day. She jumped out of bed and ran down the hall to awaken her mother. She went into the bathroom and splashed cold water on her face, and after tolerating its first shock, she stepped into a warm shower. Today was no ordinary day. She wanted this day to be etched in her memory forever.

Several miles away Chen Young was already up and dressing. He had hung up the phone after a long and stressful conversation with his parents. The plan was they would meet him at the hotel, wish him well, and proceed to the brunch Sarah had planned for the guests. "The hotel is seven miles off the turnpike." He warned them to be careful not to miss their exit. Butterflies began to churn in his stomach as he anticipated the events of the day.

The nuptials were set for 4 p.m. at the Riverside Christian Church. Niki and Sarah had attended church there for nearly eight years. Chen agreed to a small reception scheduled after the service. A few of the lingering fall leaves still provided a hint of color. The sprawling lawn, situated behind the church, had been manicured by a few volunteer congregants.

They managed to transform it into an ideal setting for the couple to celebrate their union. All those who knew the Hughes at Riverside would be there. The pastor had provided a large tent in case the weather took a turn. The head count was 75 guests, a scarce amount of people to the Hughes family. The finest of caterers and musicians were hired, hoping the guests' evening would be a memorable one.

Niki stepped into her wedding gown, and Sarah caught a glimpse of her daughter through the mirror over the bureau. The vision startled her. She turned to her daughter, and her tears flowed freely.

"Come on, Mom. None of that," Niki scolded. "You'll have me crying, too. I need to keep my makeup intact." Sarah smiled and agreed to compose herself.

The alencon lace veil Niki chose cascaded from a padded satin hanger attached to the top of her closet door. She had unfolded a clean sheet and placed it on the floor under the veil in case it should settle and drop. Sarah helped her arrange the veil securely to complete the ensemble. The church service would not commence for several hours, so Niki undressed, satisfied the vision in the mirror was as she had envisioned it since she was a teenager. She gently hung the gown and veil back in place and arranged her hair.

Four of Niki's friends from church were selected to be her bridesmaids. Her Matron of Honor Amy had been her friend since high school, and they continued their friendship beyond college at a Bible school not far from the university. Amy moved to a small town about fifty miles away, married, and had two daughters Rose and Christine. They managed to keep in touch, speaking often. Her entourage, Susie, Gladys, Linda and Virginia, had already arrived and settled down in the church basement to pass the time by sharing stories since they had last seen each other and sipping coffee out of plastic cups. Another sister in Christ Luciana was running a bit late. She would sing the Our Father at the ceremony. The day was planned—4 p.m., the Nuptials, 5 p.m., Photographs, 7 p.m., to 10 p.m., the reception on the back lawn.

The chefs of a local restaurant were busy preparing the food. It was to be delivered in their truck while the church service was in progress. On the two-acre lawn the rest of the staff were setting up tripods, in neat rows, on long tables with fuel burners beneath them where a variety of food trays would be placed.

Sarah excused herself and left Niki to finish her last-minute preparations. Passing through the kitchen, she retreated to a corner of the back porch, her respite. Blanketed with brown and yellow leaves, she sat on the weatherworn Adirondack rocker and gazed out at the late fall grass. It reminded her of a warm quilt. She smiled. Resting her head back, she began to rock. She thought of all the triumphs and sorrows, the loneliness in making the hard decisions that would affect her daughter's life, and the happiness she had knowing the Lord was her Confidant, her Best Friend, and even her Lawyer. *Doesn't the Word of God say this?*

Sarah had grown up in the early 50's. A great time to grow up in, she thought. The war was over, and the returning soldiers had settled in small communities to raise their families with some of the world's problems behind them. She was a baby boomer. It was a time when bobby socks were fashionable along with drive-in movies, sock hops, saddle shoes, poodle skirts, and egg creams. It was a time when a teen could ride the bus alone to Main Street, USA, meet her friends, enjoy a movie, visit the local record shop, and end the day with a banana split or kitchen sink at Josie's Ice Cream Parlor without worrying about being abducted or raped. It was a safe time, and although the draft was still being enforced, many young men who remained on the home front went to work for their living and opted out of college to help with family finances. These same young men could be seen on the weekends proudly driving their used Chevy Bel Airs or Thunderbirds with wrap around windshields. She remembered how the whitewall tires beamed in the sunlight. Some cars had special sounding horns that echoed through the streets on a warm summer night. To her, it was a wonderful time—it was a time of peace.

Sarah reminisced in detail about the day her friend, Anita, received a silver convertible as a birthday gift from her parents. She had turned eighteen and eager to drive. She invited Sarah to take a trip to the Catskill Mountains in upstate New York. She remembered the huge pines that were so tall they seemed to reach into the heavens. She could still smell their fragrance. She never forgot the adrenaline rush she felt as she gazed through the rear-view mirror and saw only the darkness that enveloped them. A feeling of total abandonment came over her. As the years passed, the same feeling would overcome her at times until she accepted Christ into her life. She has since relied on His promise He will never leave or forsake her.

Sarah closed her eyes as she rocked and began to drift off. The images of the past slowly faded, and she fell into a deep sleep for at least an hour.

"Mom, wake up." Niki shook her mother's arm.

"Good Lord, I've drifted off. Haven't I? Are you satisfied with your dress?"

"No last minute alterations needed," Niki said. "My dress is everything I hoped it would be."

Both women smiled as they greeted the flow of relatives and friends for the early brunch. Chen, not wanting to see his bride before the church service, opted to have a late breakfast sent to his hotel room. His parents arrived thirty minutes late. Chen's Aunt and Uncle followed behind them. The Young family embraced the two women upon entering the restaurant. "My son warned us to pay close attention to the road signs," Mrs. Young said regretfully." We didn't." Everyone laughed.

"Not to worry, the main thing is you are all here." Sarah smiled and ushered them to their seats at the head table. The groom's family remained cordial throughout the early afternoon. They mingled with Niki's relatives and commented on the excellent choice of food. They were blessed and hoped this day would be a memorable one for them and the future bride and groom.

Sarah was seated next to the Youngs at the Reception. They were comfortable enough with her, and the other guests, to speak freely about their life in the Orient. She was curious about Chen's past and this gave her the opportunity to learn about their son's upbringing in China. His father revealed he had spent most of his teenage years in Hong Kong. He spoke fluent Cantonese and learned English in primary school. Late into his teens, he was sent to live with his aunt and uncle, in the northeastern part of the United States. He applied to several colleges and was accepted into Bridge State College, where he received his B.A. degree in Criminal Justice. Training at the Police Academy followed. He was hired by the Camwood

Police Department soon after. They had remained in Hong Kong, and his aunt and uncle were his only living relatives in North America. Leaving his parents was difficult. China was coming into its own, but some smaller industries were still being run by the government. This became a red flag to the Youngs, and they decided after much deliberation to seek a safe haven in the States. They followed several years later, migrating to the United States and leaving their past behind.

The Youngs were practicing Buddhists. After their son's conversion to Christianity, they noticed a significant change take place in his life. He seemed more responsible and caring. A definite change for the better. Up until that time, they would have never accepted his choice of a soul mate.

It had been a slow process for Chen as the Lord chipped away, sculpting his heart of stone into a heart of flesh. His parents started to question their own beliefs. After weeks of quiet talks, they approached Chen and asked him to explain the precepts of his faith in Christ. Why was a Savior needed? Do you have to be a good person, following the rules of your religion, to earn a place in the afterlife? They discussed this in the Cantonese language. Chen obtained several Christian tracts explaining the gift of Salvation in their native tongue. He had left the literature with them on his last visit. He knew all he could do was pray the Holy Spirit would open their minds, and their hearts, and reveal Himself to them. After much prayer to "the one who created us," their understanding of God's plan for the world became vivid. "Yes, we need a mediator to intercede between God and man." "Yes, we all need His forgiveness." The way of the Cross became clearer to them; so clear they stopped attending temple altogether, and Sunday service at a local church became their priority.

It was on this special day the Youngs decided to tell Chen of their commitment to Christ. They knew it would be a gift that would surpass all other tokens of love and beauty the young couple could receive from them. They chose a time before the ceremony while they were waiting for the bride to arrive.

Chen was in the vestibule of the old Pentecostal Church. He was straightening the white carnation that hung sideways in his lapel. In this quiet space, he caught glimpse of his parents through the large byzantine mirror on the wall. He swung around and embraced them. "You made it ok—didn't get lost this time?" He chuckled.

"Yes, Son, we made it fine." All three spoke in their native language.

Chen sensed a change in his mom and dad's countenance. Their beaming faces revealed to him they were hiding a deep secret—a wonderful, enlightening secret they were about to reveal only to him.

"What's gotten into you two?" Chen asked. "What are you up to?"

"Can we go sit over in the corner, Chen?" Mr. Young pointed with his eyes. Your mother and I have something to tell you."

Retreating to the far end of the hallway, the couple seated themselves on the long wooden bench that had welcomed thousands of church goers for the past seventy-five years. "Son, your mother and I have accepted Christ into our lives. We have been attending a church for many weeks and wanted to share this good news with you on this, your special day." That's as far as he could go before the tears streamed down his face. Chen's mother looked on silently. She, too, was crying. "Yes," she kept repeating, "Yes."

Chen, having spent his adult life in a westernized culture, had only a slight hint of his roots in his voice. On the other hand, his parent's voices revealed they came from another world. On this day, as they spoke, Chen heard them loud and clear. He couldn't have been given a sweeter gift. The Book of Acts came to his mind. When the jailer, who led Paul and Silas out of the prison approached them with the question "What must I do to be saved?" They answered a simple, "…believe on the Lord Jesus Christ and you will be saved, you and your household." Believers stand on this Scripture with confidence and through prayer, you and your household will be saved.

~ CHAPTER FORTY-THREE ~

A light rain fell on the small Island. Neva sat back in her rocker and closed her eyes. The sound of the drizzle on the tiled roof comforted her. She recalled the events of the past several weeks, as the sun shower found its way through the clouds. *This has been quite a journey.* The corners of her mouth curled upward. She reflected on all Alma had done for her. *She has been such a help to me. I must do something to show my appreciation.*

The memory of Tex no longer entered her mind—until this day. She came through the accident in her garden without serious complications but reminded herself the time she spent confined to her bed would have been unbearable without the help of her dear friend and neighbor. Both women followed Dr. Ottorro's instructions, which included bed rest and plenty of fresh air. Alma visited each day to make sure Neva took her medication on time. She did not skip a single dose. Closer than sisters, the two elderly women had shared their present thoughts and their memories for hours on end. However, on this particular morning as she rocked back and forth, she thought of the tall, dark, stranger she had met on the plane. *What happened to him? Such a dear soul.*

The familiar sound of a knock on the door interrupted her thoughts. "On time as always," Neva said in a voice loud enough for the visitor to hear. "Come on in. The door is open."

Alma appeared in the doorway and stepped into the small living room, drenched in a warm glow, illuminated by the shifting Puerto Rican sun.

"Good morning, Sister." Neva said.

"Good morning to you," Alma replied. "Coffee up?"

"Not yet, just sitting and pondering."

"Pondering what?"

"Oh, digging up some old ghosts."

"No such things as ghosts and you know it. Now sit back and relax, I'll get the coffee started."

"Thanks, Alma, I don't know why I can't get moving today. These tired old bones have taken over my willing spirit. My mind says, Neva, get up and start moving, get something done, but my bones remind me they're too old and tired to accomplish anything." They both laughed. Alma retreated to the kitchen.

The aroma of fresh brewed coffee filled the room. Alma placed the silver tray on a table next to Neva. Picking up the delicate pitcher, hand painted by a local merchant, she poured a small amount of milk into Neva's cup before adding the coffee.

"Why do you do it that way?" Neva raised her voice.

"What's the difference which way it's done? It still comes out the same in the end," Alma retorted. "Next time do it yourself." The two ladies were off and running. *She must be better.* She cracked a half-smile, "besides it's easier to measure the milk that way."

The morning wore on and the ritual continued. They chatted and argued, oblivious to anything else. Their conversation started off light, touching on the weather, the latest news, and what suit to wear to the church service on Sunday. Then Alma's thoughts shifted. "As you know, my nephew sends me the local papers from the States, from time to time. I was breezing through the pages yesterday, and I came across a photo of a man that resembled the gentleman who you met on your last trip home."

"How do you know what he looked like?" Neva asked.

"I must confess. The night he came over to take you out to dinner, there was a nosy neighbor peeking through the blinds."

Neva's eyes widened. "So, up to your old tricks of snooping. Hey?" Alma decided this would be the perfect opportunity to needle her friend. With a twinkle in her eye, she leaned toward Neva. Her nose crinkled as she raised her voice. "He was so tall and handsome. I couldn't take my eyes off him." Seeing she wasn't ruffled in the least, her demeanor changed. "I'm sure it's not him, but the resemblance is striking."

"Go on."

"This man was arrested on conspiracy to commit murder."

"Murder!" Neva nearly jumped out of her seat. "Murder who?" Her feeble hands began to shake. "Alma, you go home and bring me that article at once," she demanded.

Alma turned ashen. In all the years they were friends, Neva had never spoken to her in that way. Seeing her distress, she walked over to her friend and gently patted her hand. "I'll be back in a jiffy, Dear."

As she waited, Neva thought back to the kind gentleman that not only carried her luggage off the plane but the man who had become her friend, visited her, and took her out for "a night on the town." She put her rocker in high gear. "Not him," she said aloud, "not him."

It took several minutes for Alma to return with the newspaper in hand. "Here." She handed the wrinkled paper to Neva. She tapped her index finger on the image of a tall, dark, man, being led out of a motel room in handcuffs by two police officers. A police car could be seen several feet away. "Here," she repeated, "see for yourself." The pounding began in Neva's chest and rose to her ears. Her head began to throb, and she felt feverish. Noticing the sudden change, Alma sat her back in her chair. "Take a few minutes before you speak," she told her.

Neva gazed at the photo. She silently prayed her eyes were deceiving her. She wanted to deny the image before her was that of her new acquaintance. She could not.

"What do you think? Is that him?" Alma asked.

Still speechless, Neva adjusted her reading glasses and began to read the article. "A Texas ex-con was taken into custody yesterday for violating parole and was being held on a charge of conspiracy to murder an Arizona widow." Neva gasped. She could not go on. "Go get my pills, Alma," she instructed.

"Which ones?"

"All of them, you know where they are."

"Neva, it's not time."

"Get them. I'm not waiting until one o'clock. I want to take them now."

Knowing not to argue with her, Alma obliged. She returned with the pills and placed them on the side table. Diverting her attention, she handed Neva her coffee cup.

After the first sip, Neva winced. Alma sensed its contents had turned cold. "Can I reheat this for you, or do you want me to finish reading you the article first?"

"Read." She laid her head back and focused on the ceiling. Alma continued where Neva had left off: "Thomas, aka Tex, Black, was arrested by the Houston Police Department and questioned about his involvement in the recent shooting of a Phoenix widow. Based on a statement from an ex-cellmate who was taken into custody for the crime, the cellmate Lou Parisi, also known as Louie Paris, has implicated Black as part of the conspiracy. His accomplice Frank "Mo" Digbey has also been arrested. The details of their motives have not been released. No further information has been given to the media." Neva held her chest and looked directly into Alma's eyes. "Yes, Alma, that's him."

"When I think of what could have happened to you. That's what you get when you trust a stranger — you could have been killed," Alma admonished. Detecting tears in Neva's eyes, she stopped speaking.

"I was fond of that young man," Neva cried. "When he disappeared without a trace, I wondered what had happened to him — even prayed for him."

"You can keep praying," Alma said. "He'll need those prayers."

She resumed her task of straightening up the kitchen and returned to the living room. She checked the time and handed Neva her pills and watched her swallow them. "I must be going, Dear. You rest up and give a ring if you need anything." Her smile was reassuring. "Same time tomorrow?" she asked.

"Yes, God willing, same time."

Alma approached the door, and Neva called out to her. "You've been so good to me. I want to do something for you — something special. Depending on how we are both feeling, would you like to take a trip with me? There's a little place I'd like to take you to, and I think you would enjoy it. It's tucked away in a small village across a river where no one can find us even if they tried."

Alma looked back at her friend and smiled. Before she could answer, Neva slapped her hand onto the coffee table. "Then it's settled," she cried out. "We are going on vacation."

~ CHAPTER FORTY-FOUR ~

The fragrance of freshly baked croissants permeated the kitchen and snuck its way into the adjoining rooms and up the stairs. Adelaide set her alarm an hour earlier the night before, so she could have an early start. All the prideful thoughts she ever had culminated in her baking skills. After all, she had won the baking contest at the Camwood County Fair for three consecutive years, and she knew no one could whip up a croissant as flakey, puffy, and buttery as she could.

George Asher had been patronizing the Purple Cottage Bed and Breakfast, for at least a decade. His favorite part of the day was breakfast. Adelaide put out a spread, second to none, and he was not about to miss this one. "Adelaide, you outdid yourself this morning," George said. "Along with everything else, I didn't expect fresh sausages this trip. The coffee alone is worth getting up for."

"How long will you be staying this time, George?"

"To be honest, I'm just passing through. My business has taken me elsewhere this trip. However, I had to stop in Camwood, I missed your good cooking, and I missed seeing you." There was a twinkle in his eye.

"I hope my niece was courteous to you when you checked in last night." She avoided his eyes. "I had to run several errands. I had no choice, except to have her hold down the fort for a few hours."

"She was more than courteous. She went out of her way to make me feel welcome. Have you been busy enough, Adelaide?"

"The summer was busy. The way the economy is nowadays I suppose it wasn't busy enough. I shouldn't complain though. I'm meeting my bills."

Adelaide placed a large dish of eggs, sausages, fresh fruit and warm croissants before George and poured a fresh brew into his cup. She politely excused herself, leaving him to delve into his favorite meal. She walked up the old kitchen stairs, entered her bedroom and shut the door. She stopped at the window to take in the fresh morning air. A tear found its way down her cheek and onto her collar. No one of the opposite sex had ever paid much attention to her before, and the words, "I missed seeing you," George spoke, took a toll on her emotions. Some of the young people in her town referred to Adelaide as "the old maid." The older generation that knew her admired her. They had accepted the fact she was the nice lady that ran the B&B, the woman that would never marry and have a family of her own. Her nieces and nephews adored her, and she made them a priority in her life, but it didn't make up for her loneliness. The fact George showed even the slightest interest in her had thrown her off. She pushed her feelings for him back into her brain for years. She thought no one cared, much less George.

George Asher was the rugged type. He traveled often for his insurance company. His tall muscular build would make one think he was in another business, a blue collar one—construction maybe or some kind of mechanics. Adelaide never asked him why he chose the white-collar route. She enjoyed listening to the stories he told of his travels. She dared not expect more. On most occasions he would talk non-stop, but after years of keeping the conversation light, she did not expect this. *Am I reading too much into one small statement, one expression of caring?*

Adelaide washed her face and dried it with a fresh washcloth. She touched up her makeup, applied the foundation carefully, and added some red lipstick to her lips. Descending the stairs, she returned to the dining area only to find it empty. Darting into the foyer, she opened the large book resting on the old oak table. In the past, she had chosen to record her guests arrival in some old unused ledgers she had found in the attic when going through her father's belongings. She opted out of the usual registers used by most hotels and inns. It was a challenge for her to fit all the information needed with the vertical and horizontal lines getting in the way, but she had her own system of recording the arrival dates. The guests would sign their names on the longer lines. After they departed, she would put a smiley face sticker in the column next to the visitors she enjoyed in hopes they would return for another stay. She repeated the ritual for any newcomers. Of course, it didn't include her regulars, such as George. The smiley face for him was imprinted in her memory. The ledger had been missing. Puzzled, she thought she may have misplaced it and was searching for it in her spare time. Turning to the last evening's entries, she found George's name and time of arrival: George Asher, Arrived Sept. 1, 7 p.m. Leaving Sept. 4, 11 a.m. "Thank, God, he's staying an extra night," she whispered. Her grin widened as she contemplated an extra day of seeing him.

The weeks passed. The morning was crisp. The northeastern sun streamed through the openings of the white eyelet curtains. Its rays shined down on the welcoming spread which Adelaide had envisioned. Knowing this day would be a busy one, she had awakened early. She showered and dressed and found her way through the darkness and down the stairs into the kitchen to create a small feast for her newly arriving guests. Walking over to the chafing pans, she lit the cans of fuel in the bottom rack and set them in place to keep warm.

The B&B was booked for the weekend. Her guests were to arrive at different times. Weary after the long preparation, Adelaide pulled out a wooden chair from its place at the table and grabbed the pot of steaming decaf. She poured the brew into a china cup which she had set in line with the others. *I'll replace it.* She picked up the morning paper lying in a vacant spot among the blue and white place settings. Gleaning over the advertisements and coupons the Daily Gazette offered, she turned back to the first page headlines that had caught her eye. "Camwood's Own Arrested on Drug Trafficking Charges." She read. "Joseph Balboa, a long-time member of the Camwood Police Dept. was brought into custody last night on allegations of accepting bribes from Chinatown dealers. According to sources within the department, the officer had been living a double life for several years. The department is not offering any more information on the arrest. A thorough investigation is being conducted of all department personnel.'"

Joe Balboa and Adelaide had been friends for many years. The police officers would stop by often, on the night shift, to pick up any muffins and croissants she may have left over from the morning breakfast. They would bring the baked goods back to the station house for the others to enjoy. Adelaide called it "a gift of gratitude" for the officers keeping her and her guests safe all the years she had been running the B&B. It was not unusual when Joe called her ahead of time and asked if he could stop by.

"I'm on the graveyard shift tonight, would you mind if I came later than usual," Joe had asked.

"I'm going to bed soon, I'll leave the latch unlocked and you can lock up on the way out. The muffins will be in a bag on the kitchen counter."

As she finished reading the article her eyes turned to saucers. "Oh my Lord, who would have thought...."

The sound of voices in the vestibule interrupted her. Jumping up, she folded the newspaper, smoothed the ecru lace tablecloth, and hurried into the entrance hall to greet her guests.

The first to arrive was Neva Pelleron and her neighbor Alma Pearson. Neva, as chipper as ever, hugged Adelaide so tight she had to gasp for air. A much weaker hug by Alma followed.

Adelaide was meeting Alma for the first time although Neva had spoken of her many times. After a short introduction, she showed the two women to their rooms and reminded them other guests would be arriving shortly. "I've prepared a special brunch," Adelaide said. "Don't forget to check in," she reminded them. "I can't figure out what happened to my old ledger. Please sign into the new book whenever you're ready."

Since they both snored, Neva and Alma decided not to share a room. After each one settled into their havens of Victorian history, they descended the stairs to the parlor. They chatted away for at least half an hour and filled Adelaide in on their lives in the tropical Island they called home.

The phone in the hallway rang, and Adelaide excused herself. The two ladies, who were within earshot, could hear she was talking to a gentleman. Neva fired a look at Alma and smiled. Alma caught on and smiled back.

Adelaide was ecstatic. "How wonderful, George. How soon can you be here? My other guests will be here soon, and I would love for you to meet them."

Adelaide had been seeing George for over a month, and their relationship had blossomed. She had gone to bed many nights with grateful tears. God had provided her with a good man. She anticipated their future together knowing the love and respect he showed her would never wane. He was her soul mate.

Adelaide returned to the parlor but was interrupted by noises in the entrance hall. She excused herself, leaving Neva and Alma alone. As she entered the hallway, she was greeted by the Heatons—Jack and Anne. "So nice to see you again, Jack, and who might this be?" She turned to Anne. "I see you have a new member of the family."

"This is my wife Anne," Jack beamed. "We're expecting our first child next summer."

"Congratulations. I'm pleased to meet you, Anne." She walked over to her new acquaintance and gave her a hug. Trailing behind as usual, Sean had just walked in the door and looked two inches taller. "Sean, will you ever stop growing?" she teased. All four laughed.

Adelaide escorted the family upstairs to their rooms." This is your room, Sean." She opened the door to the left of the hallway.

"Cool!" Sean eyed the lap top computer on the desk under the window, complete with two speakers and a printer. He dropped his suitcase on the floor and leaped onto the bed.

Adelaide ushered Jack and Anne into the larger suite, next to Sean's room. "Now you two settle in, and I'll meet you downstairs. Brunch is ready, and there are a few guests I want you to meet.

What a beautiful morning, Marge thought, as she climbed into the airport taxi. After several weeks of therapy, her coordination and balance returned. She thanked God the bullet she took was not fatal. When the swelling of her brain tissue had subsided, she was able to begin her rehabilitation, and she was successful in reaching the goals set for her. Taking one last look at the sky, she gave a long audible sigh, sat and shifted her weight until she was comfortable.

"Anything wrong, Ma'am?" The driver slammed the door shut.

"I was taking in some air," Marge replied.

"I can open the windows for you, Ma'am."

The offer went unnoticed—her memory jarred by visions of Harry and the events that followed on her last trip to the Northeast.

She could hardly believe she was returning a widow, one who would lose almost everything her husband had worked for, including the good name he so foolishly tarnished with extortion.

"Where to, Mrs.?" The driver asked.

She was grateful for the interruption. "Camwood."

As the taxi whisked through the narrow streets, Marge got a glimpse of one of the canals. It reminded her that her destination was near. She opened her handbag and fumbled around until she found the small tapestry purse that held her spare bills and change. The driver slowly brought the cab to a halt. She handed him the price of the ride and a generous tip.

"Thank you, Ma'am. Enjoy your vacation." He proceeded to walk around and open the door. Offering his hand, he helped her exit the taxi. He circled around the car and removed her suitcase from the trunk. "Can I bring in your bag?"

"No, thanks, I can manage." Marge was not ready to walk into the B&B. Another quick goodbye found her standing there alone with her suitcase at her side. Looking straight ahead, her eyes focused on the soft color of the purple door, adorned with a wreath of white hydrangeas that hung over its stained glass window. A familiar feeling came over her. She stood staring for a moment, and her loneliness began to fade. She knew this was one place she would be welcome despite the events of the past.

The media had had a field day as they delved into Harry's past. The bank statements in Europe and Canada were all traced back to Harry Bernside. Filtrec Electronics Corp. suffered a great deal from the publicity, and their stocks plummeted. Thousands of investors wanted to sell fast since they now associated the company and the CEOs with extortion and money laundering. Of course, it was all a fallacy, but try telling them. Most of the stockholders outside the company wanted out yesterday. Marge had been hit hard. She was able to keep the house, and there was enough money to pay back the government for all the back taxes Harry, Sr. owed. There was little left. Her husband's pension was still in question, and Marge had to rely on his Social Security checks for income. The government had confiscated all of his foreign accounts which they found untouched. The rainy day he was saving the money for still puzzles Marge.

Adelaide was busy in the kitchen when she heard the bell. Rushing into the foyer, she greeted her guest. "Welcome Marge." She grabbed both of her hands. "Let me take that for you. I've been expecting you." She lifted Marge's suitcase. "Come in and make yourself at home. Some of the other guests have arrived."

Since she last saw her, Adelaide was aware of the happenings in Marge's life. The story did not go unnoticed by the small-town newspaper. The Daily Gazette saw to it. They gave it full coverage, and she was determined to help Marge through this adversity by making her trip as pleasant as possible.

Marge found it difficult to smile. She remained silent and followed Adelaide to her room. "I'll be down shortly," she told her. Adelaide hugged her and left her to unpack.

After emptying her suitcase, Marge sat on the edge of the bed and began to weep. *What other guests. Do they know about Harry?* She was unable to pull herself together. She pressed her face against the pillow, and her soft cries turned into deep sobs. She lay there for at least twenty minutes before she started to drift off into a long-awaited sleep.

Downstairs, Jack and Anne were anxious to see who had arrived. "Where's your latest guest?" Jack placed his arm around Anne. Sean, who had slipped out the back door, was nowhere to be found.

"She'll be down shortly." Adelaide knew Marge would have a difficult time making an appearance; she changed the subject. "Where is your son?"

"I think he's out in the courtyard throwing some basketballs."

Adelaide excused herself. "I have to attend to my cooking." She entered the kitchen and used the back staircase. She found her way to Marge's room. By this time her guest had freshened up, changed her clothes, and approached the main stairs. Finding her guest's room empty, she caught up with Marge, who was halfway down the steps that lead to the foyer. "I'm so sorry, Adelaide, for taking this long."

Adelaide smiled, *thank God, at least it's a start*.

Entering the parlor, Adelaide presented Marge to the waiting guests. "Do you remember me?" Marge asked Jack.

"Of course, I remember you. It's good to see you again."

Marge tried hard to smile, wondering how much he knew. Then she glanced at Anne who caught her puzzled look. "I don't believe we've met," Marge said.

"I'm the newest member of the Heaton family," Anne said proudly. "Our son Sean is out back I believe." Unable to contain her excitement, she announced, "We are adding a new addition to the family next summer."

"Congratulations on your exciting news. I remember your son. I imagine he's grown taller since I last saw him."

"You'll have plenty of time to see Sean. You might not recognize him. He has grown as you've imagined," Jack's grin widened.

Marge turned to Neva Pelleron. "How are you, Neva? We had a nice talk together in the past. I hope we can do it again this trip."

"I'm sure we will," Neva turned to Alma." This is my dear friend and neighbor Alma Pearson. We've been through a lot together, so I thought we deserved to get away from it all." She chuckled. "We're looking forward to a nice quiet vacation. I know we'll have a lot to share since we've last seen each other."

Marge smiled at Alma and shook her hand. She walked over to the oversized wing chair next to the fireplace and sat. All eyes were upon her, and she examined the expression of each guest who was to be her housemate for the next few days. She forced a timid reply. "Yes, a lot to share."

~ CHAPTER FORTY-FIVE ~

After saying goodbye to their parents, the newlyweds changed their clothes and left for the airport. The wedding couldn't have been lovelier. Niki was a married woman now, and after keeping a list of goals she had set for herself, which hadn't included marriage, all her priorities shifted. She and Chen were both aware they would have to compromise and meet halfway at times. After being single for so long, they were willing to make the adjustments.

As they drove toward the interstate, Niki started to have second thoughts. "Do you really want to fly to Canada tonight, Chen."

"Why? What are you thinking?"

"I have always wanted to see more of the States. Could we switch our tickets for a later date and drive west? Let's see where it takes us. I brought some maps with me and I would love to see that part of the country. Would you mind very much?"

Chen knew he must be flexible at times, but he didn't expect to be challenged so soon. He began to mumble.

"What are you saying? I can't hear you."

"I'm praying." He laughed.

"Asking, or thanking God? You haven't answered my question."

"I don't want to begin our life together with an argument. What brought about this sudden change?"

Niki opened the glove compartment and retrieved the maps she had placed there before the wedding. She took a highlighter and began to outline a route, beginning in the North and ending at several western states.

"We have three weeks," Niki reminded Chen. "We could cover several spots of interest. There's one thing I want to do before we head west. I want to stop and see Adelaide and surprise her. You haven't met her yet. She couldn't make the wedding, and I know she would be thrilled to meet you. We don't have to stay long."

Chen smiled. He pulled into the nearest gas station, filled the tank, and drove in the opposite direction.

Grateful for her first victory, Niki leaned over and kissed Chen on the cheek. He laughed as the SUV sped toward the small village he had called home for so long.

With the wedding behind her, Sarah settled back into a quieter life. After spending the morning going through a ton of paperwork, neglected mail, and the usual coupons, she placed her empty coffee cup on the kitchen table and sighed. Aware even a great novel would not fill some of the empty moments ahead, she decided it was time to venture out on her own. She vowed to keep busy on her days off and to plan a getaway if she could convince her boss to give her the time off.

The forecast called for rain in the late afternoon. Sarah hurried to the lean-to in the side yard and grabbed a hand shovel. Wanting to plant the tulip bulbs she had picked up in London, she hastened to the patch of overturned dirt she had prepared a few days earlier and began placing them six inches deep and six inches apart. She was interrupted by the phone ringing in the den. Sticking the shovel deep into the dirt, she struggled to get up and was unable to reach it in time. Checking the caller ID, she saw it was Niki calling. Excited to hear from her so soon, she pressed speed dial to her daughter's cell phone. She smiled when she heard the voice on the other end.

"Mom, how are you?"

"I never expected to hear from you this soon. Is everything okay?"

"We're checking to see if you're okay."

"All is well. Where are you? At the airport?"

"No, Mom, we canceled our flight. We decided to take a few weeks and travel across country. There is so much right here to explore. We wanted to let you know our plans have changed."

"Thanks for letting me know. I would have been checking on the arrival time in Montreal."

"We're doing great. We plan on attending church during our honeymoon. We are going to head west. We should be home in about three weeks. That will give us time to settle into our new apartment."

"You'll like living in Camwood. I'm sure," Sarah said with a touch of sadness in her voice. "I'll miss you both, but I'm looking forward to the day when Chen can enter full-time ministry."

Sarah hung up the phone and wiped the tears from her face. They were happy, grateful tears. Thanking the Lord for making it all possible, she returned to her gardening. She continued to form neat symmetrical rows that would be her tulip bulbs resting place for the winter months. She hoped, in the spring, they would blossom into the array of colorful blooms she had envisioned.

The remainder of the weekend rolled around faster than expected, and Sarah found herself groping through the usual statements, bills, and coupons, but this time she included pamphlets and travel brochures. She took a few minutes and stepped onto the front porch to retrieve the newspaper, hoping to go unnoticed in her no longer white terrycloth robe. She entered the kitchen, filled the percolator with water and sat on the island stool. Scouting for bargains that would catch her interest, she found nothing. It took a few turns of the page for one column to catch her eye. It caused her to run to the window to read it in the morning light. "Could this be true?" she cried, although there was no one to answer her. She read on: "Two Camwood Police Officers Indicted for Drug Trafficking—Internal Investigation Ongoing." It went on to say that the officers were involved in a plot to murder a Phoenix housewife. The gun used in the shooting was retrieved and traced to Feldman's Pawn Shop, not far from the Sky Harbor Airport. The pawn shop had been closed, and the owner was still under investigation.

Sarah found her way to the living room with her newspaper in hand and her mind going in a thousand directions. Sitting on the sofa, she composed herself enough to finish the article. Suddenly, it dawned on her. *They finally believed Niki. My daughter was right all along. And, to think that I—*she contained the thought.

    Sarah retired to her room early that evening. She brought the travel folders with her and settled in with a cup of black orange pekoe tea. She had cleared it with her boss to take some time off and she was grateful. The wedding had taken a toll on her body, and she was weary. For nearly an hour she sifted through the many options she had but found nothing appealing. After careful thought, she sat up and threw the stack of brochures onto the nightstand. She began to chuckle and shouted with enthusiasm, "I know just where to go to spend my vacation!"

END

FOOTNOTES

CHAPTER 5 pg. 21...Psalm 3, Verses 3,4,5. Scripture taken from
THE HOLY BIBLE, NEW INTERNATIONAL VERSION (NIV)...
Copyright 1973, 1978, 1984, 2011 by Biblica, Inc. Used by permission
of Zondervan. Catalog Card Number 73-174297.

CHAPTER 25 pg. 103...Hebrews, Chapter 13, Verse 2. End of
Scripture verse take from THE HOLY BIBLE, ENGLISH STANDARD
VERSION (ESV) Copyright 2001 by Crossway, a publishing ministry of
Good News Publishers. Used by Permission.

CHAPTER 30 pg. 126...Psalm 91, Verses 1,2. Scripture taken from
THE HOLY BIBLE, NEW INTERNATIONAL VERSION (NIV)...
copyright 1973, 1978, 1984, 1986 by Zondervan, all rights reserved.
ZONDERVAN Library of Congress Catalog Card Number 73-174297.
Used by permission of Zondervan.

CHAPTER 38 pg. 157...Romans Chapter 10, Verse 14 Scripture taken
from the AMERICAN STANDARD BIBLE (ASV) Public Domain

CHAPTER 41 pg. 169...Numbers Chapter 32, Verse 23. End of
Scripture verse taken from KING JAMES VERSION (KJV) THOMAS
NELSON BIBLE. Public Domain.

CHAPTER 42 pg. 176...Acts Chapter 16, Verse 31. Scripture verse
taken from NEW KING JAMES VERSION (NKJV) copyright 1982 by
Thomas Nelson, Inc. Used by permission. All rights reserved.